VITAL SIGNS

Bodies in the English Channel spell trouble for the stubborn doctor

CANDY DENMAN

Paperback edition published by

The Book Folks

London, 2020

ISBN 978-1-913516-35-2

www.thebookfolks.com

VITAL SIGNS is the fourth book in a series of crime fiction titles featuring medical examiner Dr Callie Hughes. More details about the others, available on Kindle and in paperback, can be found at the end of this book.

Prologue

He fights and struggles, scratching and pulling, trying to free himself from the cold, cold water that keeps dragging him deeper. He kicks off his shoes, to stop them dragging him down. He is hit by something? A paddle? A person? The boat? He goes under. Which way is up? He is no longer sure. He sees a glint. Moonlight on the water? He tries to reach it but something is holding him down. He breaks free, takes a gulp of air, but is then pushed down again, losing the battle, getting weaker. So tired. He just wants to sleep. Instinct tells him to keep trying, his life depends on it, but it is too late. He has no strength left. Finally, he breathes in and water fills his empty lungs. Only then does he stop struggling completely, and allows his body and mind to drift, and the light fade. Letting go. Dying.

Chapter 1

The sun was glinting on the water and the waves lapping gently against the shore as Callie pulled herself up onto the fishing boat. It had been hauled up onto the beach like all the others, to either side, looking awkward, like fish out of water. Hastings' fleet of beach-launched fishing boats was the largest in the country and it wasn't the first time Callie had been called upon to pronounce death. The last time it was a crew member hit by a loose piece of equipment in a storm, this time was rather different.

Dressed in her crime scene protective suit, Callie knelt down by the nets to see what, or rather who, they had hauled up with the fish. It was a formality for her to check for a pulse, he had been dead a few days. Seaweed masked some of the damage to his head, but the fish had nibbled at softer, juicier bits – his eyes, lips and nose.

Finding no carotid pulse, she tried for a radial one, and again found none. She used a stethoscope to listen to his chest and crouched down, putting her face close to his mouth and nose, but as she expected, there were absolutely no signs of life, just as there hadn't been on any of the bodies that had washed up on the beaches around Hastings in the last few days. All young men, some no more than boys. All cheaply dressed. All with skins darker than white, the shades varying from the deep black of this young man, to those more indicative of Eastern Mediterranean, Asian and North African origins. All with life jackets on – badly made life jackets that had little or no buoyancy and had patently failed to do their job. Half the straps on this one had broken, leaving the semi-inflated jacket lying around the man's hips.

Having pronounced death, Callie sat back on her heels.

"Such a waste," was all she could say.

"No argument there," Detective Inspector Miller agreed as they both stood back to allow the crime scene photographer, Lisa Furnow, to get her photographs. She was easily recognizable, despite the protective clothing, by the paleness of what skin was visible and her almost translucently white eyebrows and lashes. Like Callie, Lisa seemed to have drawn the short straw and had photographed the scenes of all the bodies washed up in the last few days. It had been a bad week. A very bad week.

Having climbed down from the fishing boat, Miller and Callie walked up the shingle beach, pulling off their masks and gloves, heading to where a hastily constructed exclusion line had been set up. They could see further police vehicles arriving, and an outside broadcast van. The press was already in the town and knew that a collection of police vehicles near the seafront meant another body.

Callie pulled back the hood of her suit. Her blonde hair was tied back in a scrunchie and she checked that it was still in place, hair nice and tidy. She hated to look a mess anywhere, even a crime scene.

"How many is that now?" she asked, as if she didn't know, hadn't been counting along with everyone else.

"Eight dead, five found alive."

"Do we know how many in total were in the boat yet?" Callie asked Miller.

He stopped and turned to her, a look of sadness on his face. As always, Callie couldn't help but think it was a nice face, a bit battered by time and rugby, but still a nice face, and such lovely amber eyes.

"Twenty or thirty, depending on who you ask," he replied with a shrug. "The boat was only meant to hold fourteen."

"So, between seven and seventeen bodies still to find."

"More might have made it, swum to shore and got away." But Miller didn't seem convinced that they had and Callie agreed. The chances of finding any more alive were low to zero. "And I doubt we'll find them all."

"It's just criminal." Callie was unable to hide her anger.

"Agreed."

"And not just because people smuggling is against the law," she added. "To overload a boat like that, to give them all cheap, damaged lifebelts. To send them out to almost certain death. It's more than criminal. It's inhumane."

"No argument from me."

Once they had ducked under the crime scene tape, Callie began removing her protective suit. She scowled and turned her back as she saw a journalist taking photographs of her and Miller and was glad that they were being kept some distance away.

"With the bad weather that night, they didn't stand a chance."

But Miller was no longer listening. His attention taken by a confrontation further up the beach. Two men were arguing and it looked as if it was going to get physical.

Callie recognized the younger of the two as David Morris, a local man who worked on fishing boats whenever he could get a place on one, but probably spent more time propping up the bar in the Fishermen's Social Club. An older, portly and choleric man was jabbing a finger at Morris and shouting angrily.

"And what do you know about it?" the man shouted.

"I know more than you think," Morris responded.

"You haven't got a bloody clue."

"Really? Really? You want to bet on it?"

Whilst Miller was deciding whether or not to intervene, Detective Sergeant Bob Jeffries almost broke into a run from the car park and positioned himself between the two men, interrupting their argument.

"I need you to back off," he said loudly and firmly to the red-faced man who didn't look as though he was going to do as he was told. Callie wondered if he might try and knock the policeman over and thump Morris as well. Despite Sergeant Jeffries being smaller, and older than this angry member of the public, Callie would have put money on him winning any fight. Mainly because she was pretty sure he would play dirty. However, the situation was diffused by Miller striding over to them.

"What's going on?" he asked.

Both men looked guilty. Morris shrugged.

"Nothing." He started moving away, not keen to get into a conversation with the policemen, but the older man stood his ground.

"I hope you're not going to keep the beach fenced off all bloody day," he said, indicating the police tape.

"It's a crime scene," Miller explained. "We'll keep it clear as long as we need to."

Although, Callie thought, it isn't a crime scene, even the boat couldn't be said to be that – the crime occurred out at sea.

"Rubbish. How can it be a crime scene when there's not been a ruddy crime?"

"Someone has died."

The man chose to ignore the frostiness in Miller's voice.

"Yes, but it's accidental, isn't it? He shouldn't have been trying to get into the country, should he? Bloody illegal immigrants."

"We are still recovering the body and I'd like to ask you to move away and let us do our jobs, sir," Miller said in a tone of voice that indicated he was finally near the end of his patience.

The man backed away, slightly.

"Some of us have a living to earn, you know. I pay taxes, unlike him." He gestured at the beach where the body lay. "I pay your wages," he said as a parting shot, before turning and making his way back to the road.

"Not a nice man," Callie said as she walked up to join them.

Miller snorted.

"That's Councillor Peter Claybourne, Doc," Jeffries said. "Tosser."

"He owns the amusement arcade over there." Miller indicated a large arcade in the row of shops opposite the beach. "He's just protecting his income," Miller added, giving his sergeant a warning look. Public relations was not one of Jeffries' strengths.

"That doesn't make me like him any more," Callie told Miller.

He smiled.

"No, I didn't think it would."

* * *

It was a typically busy day in the surgery and Callie was fully focused on the problems her patients brought to her. She had no time to think about anything other than her work. Dr Calliope Harriet Hughes MBChB MRCGP DipFMS, part-time local general practitioner and part-time forensic physician for the Hastings police. She was tall and slim and always smartly dressed for work, with her straight, shoulder-length, blond hair kept neatly away from her face, and her patients, with a clip.

It wasn't until later, as she walked home up to the top of the East Hill where she lived, that she was able to think again about the tragedy of the migrant boat that had capsized in rough seas off the East Sussex coast. How desperate those men, and boys, must have been to take such a terrible risk. How awful were the lives they had left behind?

Once Callie was back at home in her top floor flat, or penthouse apartment as the previous owner had described it when selling up, she kicked off her shoes, poured herself a glass of Pinot Grigio and turned on the television in time to catch the evening news.

The reporter was standing on a part of the beach that gave a picturesque view of fishing boats hauled up onto the shingle with the black fishermen's huts in the background.

"I'm here in Hastings, on the South Coast, a small town known for daytrips, fish and chips and kiss-me-quick hats as much as for its fishing fleet. A town that is sadly used to deaths at sea but which has still been rocked by recent incidents."

He hadn't got that wrong, Callie thought.

The reporter went on to summarise that a RIB (rigid inflatable boat) filled with illegal immigrants had capsized off the Sussex coast three nights earlier. It was thought that the small, overcrowded and unseaworthy vessel had been launched from a larger one, a trawler perhaps, trying to evade the well-patrolled shorter routes to the Kent coast. The migrants had been sent off from the larger one, despite the poor conditions of that night, which showed a reckless disregard for the safety of the men. When the upturned RIB had been spotted at dawn, about a mile off the coast, the lifeboat had been dispatched and three live immigrants clinging to the sides of the ruined boat were picked up, along with a body found trapped underneath and another floating in the water nearby. Two further men had been located, exhausted from their long swim ashore, in a village further along the coast. They were thought to be a mixed group from Somalia, Iraq and Syria, but all were reluctant to talk about how they had ended up in the sea, although it was very likely that they had most recently set off from France.

"With the discovery of the eighth body of a young male this morning, local MP and shadow environment minister Ted Savage had this to say."

The television cut to Ted Savage standing outside the House of Commons. An ex-fisherman himself, ruggedly good-looking and born and bred in the town, Ted was popular with locals. His unwavering support of the fishing industry, the local hospital and a range of other causes close to the town's heart had made him a runaway winner at election time.

"The terrible events in my home town of Hastings have struck at the heart of our island nation and I have been warning the Government that it would happen for many months. This tragedy could have been avoided if they had invested more in the Border Force and the Maritime and Coastguard Agency. We need to stop these boats before they enter British waters, and turn them back. For their own sake as well as ours. The Government needs to sit up and take notice. Now. Before more bodies wash up on more beaches."

True to form, just as he finished his warning of more bodies, Callie's phone began to ring. She groaned with exhaustion, already putting on her coat as she answered the call.

Chapter 2

Two further bodies had been found along the coast between Camber Sands and Dungeness, as well as one nearer to Hastings. Aware that Callie could hardly be in two places at the same time, the police caller said that her colleague in Folkestone had been alerted to attend the two near Dungeness and Callie had been allocated the third body. According to the information she was given, it had caught in the rocks at the bottom of Fairlight Cliffs, closer to where the first bodies had washed up earlier in the week. Callie was to go to the nearest point where she could park her car at Pett Level, where she would be met and taken to the location.

Bracing herself for what would probably be a battered body, and for the fact the bodies were becoming more and more decomposed as they were found, she walked along the beach from the village where she left her car, following the constable who had been waiting for her.

The pebbles changed to boulders as they grew closer to the bottom of Fairlight Cliffs. In the fast disappearing light, Callie stumbled and tripped frequently, slipping on the seaweed-covered rocks. She wasn't alone, the constable who was leading the way was finding the going tough as well. She silently cursed the fact that the man had been washed up in such an inaccessible spot, and was glad that she had had the foresight to put on hiking boots because the last thing she needed was to sprain an ankle, or worse. The gently sloping beach at Bexhill would have been a much easier location.

Eventually she saw lights up ahead and the familiar sight of white-suited crime scene investigators. The area hadn't been fully cordoned off, because of the difficult terrain and an incoming tide, but a constable had been posted at what had been designated the perimeter, to note the names of everyone attending the scene, and to ensure they were all appropriately suited up.

Callie struggled into her overalls, overshoes, mask and gloves and checked exactly where the water had now reached. She was no expert on tides, but she knew that they didn't have long to document and collect this body before the waves came and washed any evidence away. Any evidence that hadn't already been washed away, that is. A team with a stretcher was waiting to carry the body back along the beach once they were cleared to do so. Callie didn't envy them that task.

Suited and booted, she finally approached the body, recognising the slight form of Lisa, the crime scene photographer, already finishing up photographing it. In these circumstances, Callie's presence was purely a formality. They all knew the man was dead, and that the circumstances could not be deemed to be natural. The decision as to whether it was suicide, accident or murder was down to the coroner, although he could probably rule out suicide if this was another of the young migrants whose boat had capsized.

"Hi, Lisa. What have you got for me?"

Lisa stepped back to allow Callie to see the body wedged between some large rocks.

"Could you give me some more light please?" Callie asked as she leant forward to get a closer view.

Lisa angled a floodlight so that it shone more directly onto the body.

Callie could see that it was once again a young man. The face was in poor shape suggesting it had taken the brunt of the battering against the rocks at the base of the cliffs where he had been found. Callie checked for pulses, finding them absent as expected, and listened to his chest, pushing his torn plaid shirt out of the way to do so. She was surprised to see a small tattoo of a heart on his chest. None of the previous bodies had had any artwork, none that she had seen anyway. She took a moment to look at the man. He wasn't as badly decomposed as the one she had seen earlier, but different currents, differing amounts of time in the water would do that. The strap of one of the useless life jackets they had all been wearing was still tied around his waist, but the jacket itself had been torn off.

She could feel her anger rising at the traffickers who had been so negligent with these young men's lives, as she noted the time that she had pronounced death and signalled to the crime scene manager that he was free to move the body when ready. She made notes as they shifted the body. The young man's feet were bare, just as in the case of the other body that morning. It was not unusual, as people trying to swim will often kick off shoes to stop them weighing them down. She looked round, in case some had been washed up nearby but it was impossible to see anything outside of the arc of lights. She knew that the crime scene team would check the immediate area as soon as they could, and hopefully before the tide came in, but as the body could have been there a day or maybe two, and the tide would have washed over him several times, the chances of finding anything was slight.

Although her job was done, Callie waited for them to manoeuvre the corpse onto the stretcher and she followed them as they carried it back to the carpark where a mortuary van was waiting. Callie was glad that there was only a solitary press photographer there to mark the event. Perhaps the others were still in the pub.

* * *

Saturday brunch in The Land of Green Ginger, a favourite café in the Old Town, was a standing commitment for Callie and her friend Kate Ward. A local solicitor, full-figured and dark-haired, Kate was dressed in bright summery clothes and exuded health and contentment. Callie, dressed in her usual neutral tones, felt grey and jaded in contrast.

As Kate tucked into her full English, Callie was only playing with her scrambled eggs on wholemeal toast.

"You look exhausted," Kate said between mouthfuls.

"Probably because I am."

"How many is it now?"

"Eleven dead, no, twelve now. Last night it was two near Dungeness, one at Fairlight and then early this morning another was picked up by the lifeboat. That was a fun way to start my day."

"I take it he was dead."

"Oh, yes, very dead. He was spotted floating face down by a passing yacht who radioed the position to the lifeboat HQ and they went out and collected the body. But at least it's probably the last one I'll be called out to."

"Why's that? Do you think they've all been found? Everyone else made it to shore alive?"

"No," Callie said. "I suspect very few made it to shore, probably only the two who have already been picked up and, of course, the three that were found alive with the boat. We have no real idea how many there were in the first place, but it's likely it was packed and that there will be more to find. It's just that, with the way the tides work, they will wash up further along the coast now. Or as decomp takes hold, sink out at sea."

"To be pulled up in some poor fisherman's nets."

"Like the one brought in yesterday, but if they do, I just hope they don't expect me to take a look and they go straight to the mortuary."

Callie thought that it might be a while before she ate fish again.

"So how come, if the tide is pulling them east along the coast towards Dungeness, the body you went to last night was back at Fairlight?"

"It had caught in the rocks in a pretty remote place," Callie explained. "Probably been there a day or two." Callie shuddered as she remembered. "The body was not in a good state, but a bit better than the one this morning who had been in the water all that time."

"No more details please," Kate said, holding her hand up. "I haven't finished my breakfast."

Callie decided that she had finished eating, even though her food was hardly touched. She pushed her plate away and took a sip of tea. Kate was right, even though her head told her that it was entirely within reason for the recent body to get caught on the rocks and be found further to the west, against the general eastward direction of the tide, there was just a slight niggle of doubt.

"Are you seeing Billy today?" Kate asked. "Or is he too busy fiddling with these corpses?"

Callie smiled. Her boyfriend Billy Iqbal was the local pathologist and was doing most of the post-mortem examinations of the bodies, along with his usual work. He would certainly still get the ones pulled out of the sea in coming weeks and months even if Callie didn't have to.

"I do wish you wouldn't put it quite like that," Callie admonished her friend. "Someone might get the wrong idea after, you know who." She was referring to a mortuary attendant who had been caught being overly intimate with the dead in the past.

"Sorry," Kate said but she didn't look sorry at all.

"I thought I might pop in this afternoon and see how he was doing," Callie continued.

Kate leant forward.

"If I were you, I'd have a nap first," she said, honest as ever. "So you don't look quite so tired."

Chapter 3

The mortuary was situated in the grounds of Hastings General Hospital, but set back from the main buildings and shrouded with trees. No one wants to advertise their failures, least of all doctors.

Callie entered a door to the side of the chapel of rest and took the lift down to the mortuary. It was a place she had often visited, even before she started going out with pathologist Billy Iqbal, because part of her job was to liaise with the pathologist and the coroner's officer, Mike Parton, on cases involving the police. She wasn't surprised to see Mike Parton there, he seemed to have almost lived there since the bodies started washing up on the shore. He was dressed, even on a Saturday, in a dark grey suit and black tie. He looked very much like a funeral director, which in some ways, he was.

"Morning, Dr Hughes," Mike said.

"Hello, Mike, is Billy around?"

Billy himself popped his head out of the autopsy suite door before Parton could answer. He was dressed in scrubs but wasn't wearing the protective apron, mask and visor that would have suggested he was in the middle of an autopsy. About to turn forty, still slim and athletic in build,

Billy was lucky that little grey speckled his black hair yet, although Callie actually liked grey hair on men. She felt it made them look more distinguished.

"Hi, Callie, Mike, I'll be with you both in a moment. Why don't you wait in the office? Get yourselves some coffee."

Billy had an expensive coffee maker in his office and Callie wasn't sure she knew how to work it, but fortunately Parton clearly did and set about picking out pods and making them both a cup. Callie sat down, as much out of the way as was possible in such a small room, and watched him work. Parton handed her an espresso and she cupped it in her hands, breathing deeply and savouring the delicious smell of it.

"It's been a busy week," Parton said by way of a conversation starter once they were both settled with their drinks and he had found himself a space to perch on the edge of the desk.

"I'm hoping things will get a bit less busy now that the bodies seem to be moving further down the coast," Callie replied.

"I'm hoping there aren't too many more, period."

"That makes two of us," Callie agreed.

"Make that three," Billy added as he came in to join them and slid adeptly into the small space behind his desk.

"How's it going?" Callie asked.

"Depressing," he answered, but his tone belied his words. "It's going to be another long day. I've still got two more autopsies to do, and enough paperwork to keep me going for months."

Callie had expected as much, but it was still a disappointment to hear that he was unlikely to be able to spend any time with her over the weekend.

"I don't suppose I could be really cheeky and suggest a takeaway at yours later?" he added with a cheeky grin.

Callie smiled, relieved that at least he was planning on seeing her, even if it was going to be much later.

"Of course."

Parton cleared his throat to remind them that he was there. Whilst they had made no effort to conceal their relationship, it was hardly professional to discuss their personal affairs in front of him and both Callie and Billy looked sheepish.

"The coroner would like a brief update later today, so is there anything I can tell him?" Mike took out his notepad and a pen in readiness.

"The two bodies found over towards Dungeness went to Dover, I can ring them for you or—"

"No, that's fine, I can contact them directly. I'll need to do that to get copies of all the reports sent to us, anyway." Mike made a note to do this.

"I'm just completing the paperwork on the body found by the fishing boat off Hastings yesterday. Unidentified body number eight for us. All very much in line with the others. Male, IC3, late teens early twenties, poorly nourished. Cause of death: drowning."

"Any identifying features?"

Both Billy and Callie knew that identifying the bodies and informing any relatives was going to be a big part of Parton's job, working along with Miller and his team, and that it wasn't going to be easy. None of the bodies had so far had any identification on them, and few had any particular features that would make them easy to identify.

"Nope, sorry. Lisa came by and took some photos of his face, like all the others, but it's going to be hard."

Parton nodded, resigned to this answer.

"The coroner has been in touch with various groups working with immigrants both here and in France, in the hope that they might be able to help," Parton told them.

"Has anyone got in touch with the police to suggest names? Relatives who knew they were going to try and make it across?" Billy asked, but Parton shook his head.

"This isn't the same as that case where all the group in the back of the lorry were all from Vietnam and it had been pre-arranged. This is people from different countries who have probably been in Calais or France somewhere, for quite some time. Any relatives they have may not have had contact with them in recent months or even know where they are."

Sadly, Callie knew he was right, but it would have been nice if someone could identify them quickly.

"We're probably going to have to go through the Red Cross. Try and enlist their help to identify them," Parton added and Billy nodded his agreement.

"What about DNA?" Callie asked Billy. "Can't you get more detail on where they came from?"

"Sure. We can narrow it down to the main regions they are likely to have originated from, like North Africa or Eastern Mediterranean. But people move around, and more detailed analysis of where they have lived using minerals and such-like, is harder and time-consuming."

"Not to mention expensive," Parton added.

Callie knew he was right and that they might not get funding to do more tests, at least not any time soon. It would be an option held back until all other avenues had been explored.

Parton left, having extracted promises from Billy that he would complete the post-mortems on the two remaining bodies and have preliminary reports ready for the coroner by Monday.

"Well, that pretty much puts the kibosh on any plans we might have had for the weekend," Callie said morosely.

"Sorry," Billy said with a smile. He knew Callie understood, she was as much of a workaholic as he was.

Jim, the mortuary technician approached the door. Jim was slim to the point of skinny and was big on tattoos, short on teeth. He was also one of the best technicians around.

"Hi, Doc." He nodded at Callie before turning to Billy. "Next one's ready for you. Body number nine."

Callie stood up, recognising her signal to leave.

"Unless?" Billy asked.

"Unless what?" she asked.

"You could stay and watch," he suggested.

"That's quite an unusual suggestion for date night," Callie replied, with a smile on her face.

"I'm an unusual kind of guy." He waggled his eyebrows in a bad Groucho Marx impersonation.

Callie didn't need to be asked twice. She had felt an almost personal connection with this body since pronouncing death, and she wasn't really sure why. She hurriedly donned scrubs in the changing room, and went through to the autopsy suite where Billy and Jim were ready and waiting for her.

Callie's godfather had once been pathologist at Hastings Hospital, and she had watched him perform hundreds of post-mortems as he tried, in vain, to persuade her to follow in his footsteps. She had never been tempted, but she always felt a slight pang when she thought of him and how he had died so horribly in the autopsy room she was now in.

All thoughts of the past were quickly dispelled once Billy started speaking for the dictation machine, first giving a general description of the exterior of the body.

"The body of a well-nourished male. Skin tone slightly darker than IC1." It was notoriously hard to be definite about ethnicity by colour of skin alone; even alive, it was hard to distinguish someone of mixed ethnicity from say a Mediterranean, North African or West Asian background. After death, it was even harder, so pathologists would rarely say anything definite on the subject.

In the bright lights of the autopsy suite, and with his cuts cleaned, Callie took a good look at the face which she could finally see more clearly. He was a good-looking boy, she thought, or rather, he had been once.

"Age" – Billy paused to look closely at the body – "approximately eighteen to thirty years old by appearance."

Callie knew he might be able to narrow it down more when he looked at bone development and other markers visible on X-ray. All he could really say for now was that this was an adult male.

Billy continued his exterior examination and then paused while Jim measured the length of the body and read out the finding.

"One metre seventy-five."

Callie mentally converted that to five feet nine inches.

Billy went round the body checking for any external signs and describing the various cuts and bruises. He noted the tattoo of the heart, and Jim photographed it as it might help with identifying this particular body.

Billy signalled to Jim to help him turn the body over.

As soon as they had done that, they both stopped and stared at the man's left calf. Callie leant forward so that she could see what they were both staring at, as Jim reached for his camera again.

There was a tattoo on the back of the young man's leg. It depicted a cockerel standing on top of a ball and had the letters THFC below it.

* * *

After she had left him to finish up the two post-mortems, it was very late by the time Billy arrived at Callie's flat. He had called to let her know he was on his way, and the takeaway arrived at almost the same time. He was ravenous and it wasn't until he'd had two beers and his fill of the food that he sat back and relaxed.

Callie desperately wanted to ask him about the post-mortems, but didn't, thinking that he probably wanted to forget all about work. But he knew her too well, knew she would be itching to hear his news.

"So, no further surprises. I am sure that both of them drowned. As you saw, body nine had a lot of bruising and damage consistent with him having been bashed against the rocks for a tide or two."

"But the tattoo?" Callie asked hopefully.

"Yes, that really was the only surprising finding."

"It can't be usual for someone from Syria or wherever to have a tattoo of the crest of Tottenham Hotspur Football Club on their leg."

"I don't know. A lot of people support Premier League clubs around the world."

"I thought that was mainly Manchester United."

"Yes, that's probably quite true, they are probably the most widely followed, but other clubs are, as well, and it may be why he chose to come here."

Callie wasn't going to be put off that easily.

"It seems a bit of a coincidence. I mean, it's got to be a possibility, hasn't it?"

"Of course. I've let Mike know and suggested the details should be checked against the UK and Interpol missing persons databases, just in case."

She was still excited by the news, even if Billy seemed less so.

"He could have been one of the smugglers," she said. "Perhaps he was supposed to steer the boat, get them safely to the shore."

"It's possible, I suppose, and in which case he didn't do a very good job."

"Have any of the others had tattoos?"

"A couple. Just bits of the Koran, that sort of thing. Nothing easily identifiable like family names."

Billy yawned.

"Well, if you've suggested they check mispers, that's the best we can do for now." She stroked his shoulder. There was no way she'd manage to get to sleep with all these thoughts whirring through her head, not unless she had something to distract her.

"Time for bed?" she asked. "Or are you too tired?"

"Never," he said, and grinned.

* * *

Callie spent a long and boring Sunday morning cleaning her flat and sorting her laundry whilst Billy was back at work writing his reports on the post-mortems he had performed the day before. Cleaning always helped Callie organise her thoughts. The repetitive and simple tasks allowed her mind to wander, and wander it did.

The tattoo on body number nine's leg bothered her, that and Kate's query about why he had been found further to the west than expected. Her glib explanation that he must have been caught on the rocks and had been there a couple of days, now seemed something of an assumption.

Bathroom sparkling and fresh sheets on the bed, Callie stopped her cleaning to make a call to the incident room. She knew there would be someone there, the team were working flat out to try and find and identify the bodies being washed up, not to mention the smugglers who had left them to die.

To Callie's relief, Jayne Hales, a detective sergeant she had worked with on a number of occasions, picked up the phone.

"Hi, Jayne, it's Callie. I just wondered if I could get a couple of details for my report on the body found at Fairlight? I seem to have forgotten to get them at the time."

"Sure, fire away, Doc." Jayne was her usual helpful self and Callie quickly had the name and contact details of the man who had found the body.

"He was out beachcombing and found a little more than he bargained for," Jayne told her.

That was something of an understatement, Callie thought.

When she called him, the beachcomber sounded like he had already been drinking and Callie couldn't blame him, finding the body must have been distressing. It was always hard, even for someone like her, who was used to death.

"It was just awful," he told her. "I don't know if I'll ever be able to go there again."

Callie could sympathise with that.

"Did you walk there often?" she asked. "Before that evening?"

"Of course. That's my bit of beach. Everyone knows that."

"Your bit?"

"For detecting. Pett Level to Fairlight Cove. I'm part of a group of local detectorists, we all have our own areas, so we don't tread on each other's toes, so to speak. That was mine. I'll have to ask if I can change. Perhaps they'll give me a sandier bit, you find more on sandy bits, generally. Coins and rings and that, and it's easier going, so you can cover a larger area."

Callie had no idea that the people she often saw out on the beaches with their metal detectors were that organised, but it was probably a good thing. She was in favour of anything that reduced conflicts.

"So, how often do, did, you walk that stretch?"

"Every day, of course. You'd be amazed at what you can find."

Like bodies, she thought, only you didn't usually need a metal detector to find them.

"You had walked that stretch of coast the day before?"

"That's right. Every day."

"And the body wasn't there then?"

"No. Of course not." He sounded suitably scandalised at the suggestion. "I'd have reported it then, if it was."

Callie hesitated before asking her next question, she didn't want to upset the man after all.

"Are you absolutely sure you would have seen it? Could you have missed it?"

"Never! I am very thorough! I make sure I cover every inch of the shoreline."

Oh dear, she really had upset him.

Once she had placated the poor man, and assured him that she wasn't in any way insinuating that he was slipshod, Callie grabbed her jacket and headed down to the seafront, or more specifically, the net huts.

These tall, black-painted, wooden buildings were the traditional places for fisherman to dry their nets and were a feature of the old town. As she wound her way through the tourists taking photographs and buying fresh fish, Callie looked for Old George, a man who epitomised old Hastings and its fishing industry. He had worked on the boats from a very young age, much younger than was legal even in those days, but now in his eighties, he just sat by his hut, telling stories to anyone who would listen.

"Hello, George," Callie said as she sat on a rickety chair beside him. She had come prepared with two cups of takeaway tea, one laced with a liberal amount of sugar. She pretended not to notice when he took the cup and added a slug of brown liquid from a bottle by his side. With all the sugar and alcohol in the cup, it was a wonder he could taste the tea at all.

After ten minutes or so of polite conversation, asking about his health, his family and allowing him to tell one his interminable stories about the bad old days, Callie got down to business.

"These bodies washing up on the beach, George."

"Terrible thing that. Terrible."

"Yes," she agreed. "Well, I wanted to know about tides and things like that, and I thought you would be the person who would know best."

George always responded well to flattery, particularly from a pretty young woman, Callie knew, and true to form, he was happy to answer her questions.

"The first body to be found was at Pett Level, on the day the boat capsized." She told him and then detailed where and when each body had been found.

"No, that's not right," he said, the moment she told him about the body at Fairlight. "That couldn't happen if he went in the water at the same time as the others. On the night of the storm, the winds were veering and that's why they ended up at Pett Level, but after that, once the wind died down, the surface water travels east and the wind has been that direction, so it stands to reason, the bodies will too. All of 'em."

"Even if this one got caught on something?" Callie queried, but George was adamant, body number nine should not have been found where he was. The prevailing winds and tides meant that it should definitely have been found further to the east.

Callie felt triumphant, her instincts were right. Body number nine did not fit with the others. Now she just had to convince the police of that fact.

* * *

Billy had a standing family commitment in the evening, and Kate was busy with a new man, so Callie thought that the night was going to be a bit of a non-event as well. Still, at least she would be well-rested and prepared for Monday – always a busy day at the surgery.

As she was already in town, Callie decided to brave the supermarket and do some shopping – always her least favourite chore. It was when she was coming out of the shop, wheeling a trolley full of virtuous fruit and vegetables neatly covering the wine and chocolate underneath in case she bumped into any of her patients, that Callie saw David Morris hurrying out of a convenience store up the road, carton of cigarettes in hand.

"David!" she called out and he looked up.

"Afternoon, Doc." He sketched a wave with the hand holding the cigarettes, realised what he was doing and hastily put the offending articles behind his back. "Gotta go." He tried to hurry past her but her trolley was blocking his way and she made no effort to move it.

"I saw you at the beach the other day, when I was seeing to that poor man who had died."

David just grunted by way of reply.

"Terrible, isn't it?" she pressed him.

"Yeah. Terrible." He began to move round her, trying to escape, and Callie didn't think it was just guilt that she had caught him buying cigarettes after a recent dose of bronchitis and a promise to give up smoking. His evasiveness piqued her curiosity.

"You seemed to be arguing with that councillor chap, what's his name?" She thought for a moment as Morris didn't seem inclined to help her. "Claybourne, that's it. Peter Claybourne. You both seemed rather heated. What was that all about?"

"Oh, you know, just political differences," Morris said unconvincingly, before finally managing to scuttle round her trolley and continue on his way towards where he lived.

Once home, as Callie put her shopping away, she thought about the argument. It had seemed something and nothing at the time, but Morris's reluctance to discuss it had made her wonder if it was something more. It didn't ring true that it was about politics, unless it was about fishing. The whole town seemed to get overheated the moment the fishing industry was mentioned, particularly if anyone threw the letters EU or DEFRA into the mix. With so many in the town relying on the sea for their livelihood, it wasn't surprising, she thought.

Grabbing her laptop, Callie looked up the council website and searched for the councillor's name. She was surprised to see just how much information was available to her. She could access his attendance record, record of voting and his register of interests on the site; so she set about looking at all of them. Unfortunately, the information actually included under these headings was relatively sparse. Councillor Claybourne had attended 70% of meetings, and was on a number of committees, including the cabinet and the charity committee. In fact, he seemed more active than a lot of his colleagues. His register of interests, besides listing the amusement arcade as a property owned by his spouse, just listed a number of charities that had him on the board and the church he attended. It was interesting to note that his wife owned the arcade but not unusual, it was possibly a tax avoidance thing, Callie thought. There was nothing to suggest why he might have been at loggerheads with David Morris.

Deciding that there was nothing more of interest on the website, Callie finally gave up. Earlier in the week, she had been craving a weekend with nothing to do, but there was no doubt that she preferred being busy. She yawned. There was nothing else for it, an early night it was.

Chapter 4

Next day, after another packed Monday morning surgery, Callie was debating with herself what type of sandwich she would get once her paperwork was finished, when she came across a repeat prescription request from Anna Thompson. The request was for a salbutamol inhaler, or rather for two inhalers. Nothing unusual there as Anna was asthmatic, but Callie seemed to remember having done a similar prescription for her only the week before.

A quick check of her records showed that Anna had indeed had some inhalers prescribed then, and the week before. In fact, she had got through far more inhalers than she should have for the last few months. Not only that, but Callie saw that there was a note on her records that she was overdue for her asthma clinic review.

Callie asked the receptionist to contact Anna and request her attendance for review before any further inhalers would be prescribed and nipped out to the bakery to get a hummus sandwich before doing her afternoon visits.

As always, Callie had the best of intentions to complete her visits and be back in good time for evening surgery, but she was waylaid by a request to see a prisoner at the police station. A driver had been involved in a minor accident and refused to take a breath test at the scene, apparently because he had chronic obstructive pulmonary disease and couldn't blow into the device. It was remarkable how quickly he found he could manage it once Callie arrived to take a blood sample. Having been called out unnecessarily, Callie took the opportunity to go up to Miller's office to see if he had any more news about the boatload of illegal immigrants.

"What's up, Doc?" Jeffries asked as soon as she entered the incident room, and then laughed at his own joke. Which was just as well, because no one else had.

"I think he means, what can we do for you, Dr Hughes?" Miller said.

It was gratifying to Callie that he did actually seem pleased to see her, well, at least he managed to smile.

"I was just wondering about the body found at Fairlight? Body nine, the one with the tattoos."

"Several of the bodies have had tattoos," Miller said with a frown.

"Yes, but this one had a football crest from a British team on his calf."

"Not that unusual," Miller said defensively. "It doesn't mean that he was British."

"No, but it's possible, isn't it? Also, the place he was found. It's all wrong."

Miller just raised an eyebrow.

"I spoke with the man who found the body and it definitely wasn't there the day before."

"So what?" Jeffries said. "He spent more time out at sea, then."

"But I spoke to an expert on the prevailing winds and tides." She hoped she wouldn't have to admit that her expert was Old George. "He said there was no way the body should have washed up there, he should have been found further to the east."

Jeffries laughed at that.

"How long have you lived here, Doc? Haven't you learned that strange things happen at sea?" Jeffries was clearly determined not to take her seriously, and it seemed as though Miller agreed, because he said nothing.

"Have you tried the national missing person database?" Callie blurted out and wished she could have taken that back as soon as she said it. She could almost feel the frostiness of Miller's response.

"Of course. Funnily enough, we do actually know what we are doing. Nigel's been in charge of that." He indicated Nigel Nugent, the go-to member of the team for anything requiring computer skills, who blushed crimson as soon as his name was mentioned. Before Callie could apologise for suggesting he might not have done his job properly, Miller had turned his back and headed into his office, closing the door behind him. Jeffries wasn't any help. He was grinning at her discomfort and shaking his head in admonishment. He looked as if he was about to wag his finger at her, so she quickly turned to Nigel.

"I take it he wasn't on there?" she asked.

"N-n-no," he said, "well, not exactly, anyway."

She raised a questioning eyebrow and he continued.

"It's not that straightforward. The missing persons register is very big, goes back years and we don't know when this person went missing, or where from."

"But he only died a few days ago."

"Yes, so we narrowed the search to men reported missing in the last week. From the skeleton and teeth, Dr Iqbal has been able to give us the approximate age of the man – eighteen to twenty-four." He blushed again, realising that he didn't need to explain to Callie how pathologists worked out the age of a dead person. "And we have his height, weight and hair colour, but that still gives us over thirty possible mispers in the south east alone. More, if we make it for the country."

"But the tattoos?" she persisted.

"Don't match any of them. Not in this country, anyway. We've heard back from some of the international databases, but won't get them all for a few days yet, but it's not looking good."

Callie was disappointed.

"I suppose it was too much to hope for an easy identification."

"I've left an alert on the sites in case he hasn't been reported missing yet." Nigel seemed eager to please, as usual.

Callie sighed. She realised it was highly likely that her man had not yet been reported missing. If he lived alone, or was out of work, it might take several days, if not weeks for anyone to realise he had gone. There was also the possibility that he would never be reported missing at all. And that was always supposing he wasn't one of the immigrants from the boat, a premise for which she had no real evidence. Just a gut feeling that this body didn't fit with the others. Nothing definite that she could use to persuade Miller that she was right.

* * *

Having arrived late for her evening surgery, Callie had not managed to catch up, as no helpful patients had cancelled at the last minute or failed to show. She was running even later by the time she finished, only just managing to leave before the receptionist locked up the building.

Kate was already seated at their favourite table in The Stag when she got there, and was probably already on her second pint.

"Sorry, bit behind today," Callie said unnecessarily.

Kate had known her long enough to know that she usually was.

"Can I?" Callie pointed to the half-empty glass and Kate nodded.

"Always."

They stayed inside the pub as the evening was cool, Callie sipping her Pinot Grigio, the one cube of ice slowly melting in it, as Kate drank her beer somewhat faster, with a packet of crisps as an accompaniment. There was no need for small talk after their many years of friendship and Callie launched right into what was on her mind: the body on the beach below Fairlight.

"I can't help thinking that maybe he doesn't fit in with the others."

"You have a whole bunch of bodies being washed up, he's one more, what makes you think he doesn't fit?"

"Well, for a start, he was found further west, against the prevailing tide."

"I thought one was found at Pett Level early on, and that was where they think the survivors made it to shore?"

"Yes, but that was on the first day, or night. The bodies were then washed up progressively to the west."

"But he was caught in the rocks, he could have been there since the first day and just not been found. That's what you told me."

Kate's law training made her the ideal person to bounce ideas off of, there was nothing she liked more than acting as devil's advocate when Callie was exploring one of her more outlandish theories and Callie knew that if she could convince Kate, then there was a chance she was right.

"True, but that was me looking for reasons why he wasn't further west. I spoke to the man who found the body. He walks the beach every day and is insistent that it wasn't there before."

"Perhaps, he got caught in a different current."

"And I spoke to Old George, the fisherman. He said not. He said the body could not have washed up where it did if it had been with the others in the boat."

"Ah. Old George."

Kate wasn't going to be easy to convince.

"Yes, and then there's the tattoos."

"I agree, that's different, and more convincing for a landlubber like me, but it could still fit with him being on the boat. Did any others have tattoos?"

"Yes, one or two, but of Arabic writing, probably extracts from the Koran."

"Okay. Does Billy agree that the body belonged to an IC6 male?"

Kate's experience in criminal law meant that she was as knowledgeable as Callie about the codes the police use to identify probable ethnicity when describing a person. IC6 covered West Asian and North African ethnicity.

"Possibly. You know as well as I do that the coding is very subjective and simply relies on skin colouring. He could easily be mixed race or even South Asian."

"With bodies washing up all over the place, from a known source, there seems very little to convince me that this one particular body is different."

"I know. But he could be."

"Could be what, though?"

"He could be one of the smugglers, or have nothing to do with the boat at all."

"What do they say about not thinking of zebras when horses are more likely?"

"That doesn't mean zebras don't exist."

Kate sighed; it was clear her friend was not going to give up.

"So now you need to get some proof."

"Yes." Callie was silent for a moment before admitting, "I'm just not quite sure where from."

Chapter 5

How to get some, or any sort of proof or even corroboration of her theory that the body at Fairlight was not from the boat, kept Callie awake a large proportion of the night. She would have liked the police to go to the press with a suitably cleaned-up photograph of the young man, and ask if anyone recognised him, but she knew that was unlikely to happen as Miller still seemed to believe he came from the boat, or, at least, was connected to it in some way. Callie was convinced he was not, which then begged the question: who was he? And why had he got mixed up with the bodies of these other young men? She thought that she could try approaching Nigel, see if he could sort out a picture of the face, something not too horrific and as clearly dead as the current one they had pinned to the board. She wanted to ask Nigel whether anything further had come from missing persons, either in this country or anywhere else, anyway.

Putting that on her to do list for the morning, Callie went on to think of other ways she might be able to show that this corpse didn't fit, didn't belong to the boat, or convince herself that it did and that she could leave it alone.

Thinking about the night the body had been found, she slowly went back over the walk along the beach from Pett Level towards Fairlight. How she had approached the scene, what she had seen. The body caught between two boulders, the damaged face, no shoes on the feet, the strap of the life jacket belt. That stumped her. Why would the body have a life jacket on, or part of one, if he wasn't from the boat? The torn shirt, the tattoos. Callie knew that nothing had been found in the pockets, no handy wallet filled with credit cards or a driving licence, but perhaps there could be some clue in the clothes. They would have been removed from the body at the post-mortem, but may have been sent on for forensic analysis. She would have to check with Billy. She was quite sure there would not have been anything overtly unusual about them, or Billy would have spotted it, but there was no harm in taking a closer look. Perhaps the labels on the clothes might tell her something.

Having given herself a couple of jobs for the morning, Callie managed to finally get to sleep.

* * *

Callie's lunchtime plans were a quick sandwich and a trip to the mortuary as she had failed to get up early enough to tackle any of her to do list before morning surgery.

She was fortunate that there were not many surgery visits scheduled and having completed her paperwork she had time to check with Judy the practice nurse about Anna Thompson.

"I've made her appointment for an asthma review tomorrow," Judy told her. "I'll make sure to stress the importance of using her preventer inhaler regularly and check technique."

"Perfect," Callie replied. "If she really does need more inhalers that's fine, but let me know what you think once you've seen her."

"I did end up leaving her a spare inhaler at the desk, because she insisted that she had lost the last prescription and had none," Judy admitted reluctantly, as she could see that Callie wasn't convinced. "I couldn't leave her with nothing, in case she had an asthma attack, but I made it quite clear she had to come in tomorrow."

Callie knew she was right, but was willing to bet that Anna wouldn't turn up for her appointment. Not now she had got what she wanted. The question for Callie was how to get her in without with-holding her medication. She just had to hope that Judy's powers of persuasion were good enough.

* * *

Callie loved that Billy always seemed pleased to see her, even when he was up to eyes in work as he was today. Unlike Detective Inspector Steve Miller who often seemed to regard her as an irritant. She also loved that he never dismissed her theories, well, not out of hand like Miller did, anyway.

"Of course, he could quite easily be British, and of mixed origins, or even from a family that came from North Africa or West Asia and settled here," he answered when she asked about possible ethnicity.

"But if his DNA showed a percentage of Northern European heritage, surely it would suggest he wasn't one of the group?"

He gave this some thought.

"It would make it more likely, but not certain, because of course, it might just mean an ancestor of his had been from Europe. The problem is that people move round, they no longer stay in the country of their birth. They seek out a better life elsewhere."

As Billy's grandparents had, Callie knew.

"But could you do it?" she asked. "DNA testing might help me persuade Miller to look harder at the possibility."

"If I can get permission, I will. But what you really need is detailed analysis of the minerals and trace elements in his hair, teeth and bones. That might possibly give us an idea of where he has been living throughout his life, and, more importantly, where he has been living recently."

Callie brightened up.

"And could you do that?"

"Not personally, no, and my department head would never agree to the expense of farming it out to a lab that can. Not unless we had something definite to go on. So, let's start with the DNA analysis and see if I can persuade him to do that, or, if he won't pay, I could maybe see if the coroner will."

Callie was pleased, at least it wasn't a closed door and she knew Billy's head of department liked him and would help if he could. She just hoped he agreed, or that Mike Parton would, because she didn't think she would get Miller to agree to fund anything.

She was about to leave when she suddenly remembered about the clothing.

"What happened to the clothes he was brought in with?" she asked. "Did anyone take a look at them?"

Billy called for Jim the technician who told Callie they had gone to forensics, although they probably wouldn't have done anything with them as they weren't considered high priority, they would just be stored in case they were needed to help with identification.

"Can you remember anything about them?" she asked Jim.

He shrugged.

"Not really. Let me check my notes." He went into the changing room and came back with a notepad. "He was wearing a torn check shirt and jeans, cotton trunks, no socks or shoes," Jim told her. "From memory, they were all cheap makes, no distinctive labels."

"Nothing different from the others?"

"Nope." He shook his head. He would have liked to be more help but there wasn't anything more he could say.

"You'll need to ask forensics if you want to take a look at them yourself, Dr Hughes," he said and she knew he was right, just as she knew it probably wouldn't help even if she did manage to get the lab to let her see them.

"Maybe Mike could get more details for you. You should ask him," Billy suggested and, much as she didn't want to add to the coroner's officer's workload, Callie knew she would probably do just that. Mike Parton was the only one who could reasonably ask forensics to see the clothes now. Well, him and Miller, and that wasn't going to happen anytime soon.

Chapter 6

Mike Parton had called ahead to the forensic lab where all the clothes and other items found on the bodies were being temporarily stored. Callie and Parton were led to the cool and well-ventilated room with shelves from floor to ceiling. Along one wall there was a row of identical cardboard boxes. Each box contained the effects of one of the bodies and all the clothing had been dried before placing in the boxes, to prevent mould.

Mike and Callie both wore gloves as they opened the boxes and checked the contents. Callie didn't want to just see the clothes from the Fairlight corpse, she wanted to compare those effects to the ones collected from the other bodies as well. If she was ever going to convince Miller that this body didn't belong with the boat, she needed to find some anomaly, something that made it stand out. Both Callie and Parton took care to only open one box at a time and replace all the contents before going on to the next. They didn't want to mix them up and the administrator who had brought them to the storeroom watched them like a hawk just in case.

Most of the men had been wearing track suit bottoms or jeans, with T-shirts and cheap jackets. All bar one had been shoeless when found, and he had only had one cheap trainer left on. A box of shoes, clothes and other artifacts found on the beaches close to where the bodies had been washed up, revealed an assortment of footwear, mainly trainers and sandals, both male and female, some of which might possibly have belonged to the immigrants. There were also the remnants of several life jackets of a similar make to those found on the bodies, more than the number of bodies found, suggesting that not only had some lost theirs in the water, others might not have been wearing them at all. Those bodies might take a while longer to be found, if ever.

When Callie got to the box containing the clothes found on the body that she was beginning to think of as hers, body number nine, she carefully spread them out on the table. Parton stopped to watch her.

The red checked shirt was battered and torn, and the label was hard to make out. Callie was pretty sure it said 'Atmosphere'. She hunted out the washing instruction label on the side seam. It gave both British and European sizes and the information on the garment was in a variety of European languages.

"I think Atmosphere is one of the Primark ranges," Parton told her as he looked over her shoulder at the label.

Callie was disappointed. She knew that the make was widely available around the world, and that he could have bought or been given the shirt anywhere.

She turned her attention to the jeans. It wasn't clear if they had been damaged by the waves or if they had been artfully torn as a fashion statement. These too were of a ubiquitous make and offered no definitive evidence for Callie to take to Miller. There was nothing to distinguish her man from the others. Even a search of the pockets proved that the forensic team had missed nothing.

With a sigh, Callie gave up. This had been a complete waste of time, both hers and that of the coroner's officer.

"Sorry, Mike."

"No problem, I needed to check them anyway."

She knew he was just being polite and it made her feel worse.

As they walked back to their cars through the main reception area of the laboratory, Callie saw Lisa Furnow coming into the building from the staff parking area, looking as pale as ever.

"Hi, Lisa," Callie called across the reception area.

Lisa looked up quickly at hearing her name, and she dropped the files she was holding in. Callie and Parton hurried over to help her collect the papers that had fallen out of them.

"Sorry," Callie said as she picked up a number of what looked to be lab reports. "I didn't mean to scare you."

Lisa snatched the papers from Callie and Parton, jamming them into the files in no particular order.

"It's okay. Thanks, I'll sort it," she said, stuffing the last few sheets of paper held out by Parton into a random file and hurrying to the staff entrance door, almost dropping the files again as she swiped her ID card and pushed through the door to the rear of the building.

Parton and Callie looked at each other and Parton shrugged.

"I've seen people happier to see me," Callie said.

"Perhaps she was just in a hurry," he suggested.

Callie thought that it was more than that, but said nothing. They began to leave again but Callie stopped. She could see a piece of paper that had travelled further than most of the others Lisa had dropped, and was now under one of the chairs by the window. She knelt down and reached under the chair, trying not to think of how inelegant she probably looked, scrabbling around on the floor. The paper was just out of reach and she had to push the chair back to get to it. Finally, she got enough of a grip on it to pull it out.

Having managed to stand up again without too much of a loss of dignity, Callie turned to take it to the reception desk so that it could be given back to Lisa. She glanced at it as she walked and then stopped in her tracks.

The top of the paper had the distinctive logo of a group known as FNM. Callie had heard of the First National Movement. It was a hate-ridden group, devoted to 'keeping Britain British'. And white. The group had been behind a number of stunts that targeted immigrants. Their erstwhile leader, Darren Dixon, or Dazza as his hero-worshipping followers called him, was currently in prison having been found guilty of contempt of court. Callie thought that it was probably the least of his crimes.

The paper appeared to be a badly printed information sheet, detailing a meeting that was due to take place the coming weekend. It seemed that the death of the immigrants, or at least the 'thwarting of their plot to invade the south coast' as the leaflet put it, was a cause for celebration.

Callie, infuriated by what she read, was about to crumple the sheet up when Parton, who had got the gist of it reading over her shoulder, took it from her.

"I think Inspector Miller might be interested in this," he said. "Forewarned is fore-armed, so to speak."

Callie happily let him take the paper. She hoped Miller would be able to do something about it, preferably stop the meeting or at least throw everyone who turned up into jail, but she knew that was hardly likely. After all, they had to commit a crime first, and she knew that this group were well-versed in the law and were generally very careful to make sure they stayed just the right side of it. Dixon had been a lesson to them all.

Callie had encountered casual sexism at various points in her life, but it wasn't until she had started going out with Billy that she had ever really understood how awful and insidious racism could be. Of course, it wasn't all intentional, Billy told her. When he was working on the wards, many an elderly patient would ask where he was from and were surprised when he replied Croydon. The fact that he came from a third-generation immigrant family didn't occur to many people. Or that he belonged in the country as much as they did. He came from a medical family, his grandfather, both parents, an elder brother and younger sister were all doctors. Only one sister had rebelled and trained as a lawyer. They all paid their taxes and worked to care for people who still regarded them as 'foreigners'. Callie was amazed at how Billy managed to shrug it off, and wondered if it was part of the reason why he now worked where he did. At least the dead couldn't ask to have a white doctor.

Chapter 7

Later that night, when they stopped for a drink in The FILO, or The First In Last Out, to give the pub its full name, Callie asked Billy that very question. Did he choose pathology so that he wouldn't have to deal with people's racist attitudes?

He laughed.

"No! Not at all," he said. "I went into pathology because I find it fascinating. We can learn so much from how and why people die."

"But didn't it sometimes get to you when patients made remarks about your colour, or being a foreigner?"

"Of course, and it still does, although, you must remember, it happens far less these days than when my parents first started practising. And it wasn't just the patients or people in the street, in those days it was their colleagues too. I think that was why my mother chose general practice in an area with a large immigrant population. My father had thicker skin, and a determination to be a cardiologist. I admire him for that. Nowadays, people still may not be completely at ease with my ethnicity, but at least they know better than to say anything to my face."

Callie thought that he was putting too good a face on what must still be a problem, even if it was minor. She knew the National Health Service was a better place to work than many others, but she was sure that Billy must still encounter racism from time to time.

"I suppose it's like sexism, it's less of a problem in the NHS than elsewhere, but still very much around. Like the sexual harassment case you were involved with," he added.

Callie couldn't fault him there.

"Doesn't anything ever make you cross?"

"Of course. But things are better than they used to be, on both the racism and sexism fronts and I honestly believe it will continue to improve. Slower than I'd like, of course, but it's still moving in the right direction."

His optimism was one of the reasons Callie loved him, so it felt bad to pursue her argument.

"What about the FNM?" she asked him and his normally happy face clouded.

"Now, that lot really do get me angry. Ignorant bunch of thugs that they are."

"I'd happily chuck the lot of them in prison and throw away the key," she agreed.

"They'd just proliferate in there," he said. "Like that American gang, Aryan Brotherhood. No, you have to just ignore them. Anything you do to retaliate gives them publicity and makes the group as a whole grow stronger." He sighed in frustration. "Come on, let's go on home and think of other things, nicer things." He took her hand and she happily left the pub and the subject behind, even if she wasn't so sure she agreed with him. The FNM and movements like it, did seem to be getting stronger. Brexit, unemployment, austerity – these were the things that fed them, that made groups like FNM potent. They had reached a critical strength now, she felt sure, and ignoring them was probably no longer an option. Not if they were going to go away.

Back at her flat, Callie made coffee and Billy switched on the television.

The late news was on and a reporter was talking about another body washed up on the south coast, this one well beyond Dungeness and on the way to Folkestone as Callie had predicted, making her think again of the body that had bucked the trend of moving further to the east with the tide.

Before Callie had the chance to give that more thought, the news item cut to another reporter interviewing local MP Ted Savage.

"What's your response to the report that the boat used by these immigrants who died in your constituency may have been sabotaged, Mr Savage?" the reporter asked, shoving his microphone in the poor man's face.

"Well, now, I think it's a bit early to be talking about deliberate damage," was his measured response.

"The report suggests—"

"I'm well aware of what the report says, and what it doesn't say," Savage continued firmly. "We now know from the coastguard radar that the migrants were brought part way across the Channel in a fishing boat, and then were sent off in the RIB a couple of miles off our coast."

"Did the coastguard manage to identify the vessel that brought them across?"

"Unfortunately, not yet. The identifying transponder was switched off, but I'm sure they are working hard to track the boat."

"And the report also raises the possibility that the sides of the RIB had been cut, either intentionally or accidentally, right?"

The reporter looked as if he was going to say more, but Savage didn't give him a chance.

"I think we need to stop speculating and let the police do their job and investigate it properly. I've nothing further to add at this point." Savage walked quickly away from the reporter, before getting into a waiting car and being driven off.

The reporter turned back to address the world, but the anchor at the television studio quickly cut him off. "Thank you, Ben, now in other news, a grandmother from Durham has—"

Billy turned the television off and took the cup of coffee from Callie.

"Have you heard anything about the boat being damaged?" she asked.

"No." He shook his head. "That's news to me."

They both thought about it for a little while.

"I wonder how sure they are that it was deliberate damage and not just from being thrown against rocks and that."

"If there were definite knife cuts to the rubber, that would do it."

"Yes," Callie said. "It would. I'll talk to Mike next week, see if I can find out more."

"It's a horrific thought, isn't it? I mean, if the boat was cut so that they wouldn't reach land safely? That's cold-blooded murder."

Callie had to agree.

∗ ∗ ∗

As she lay in bed in the early hours of the morning, mind working overtime, Billy snoring lightly by her side, she made a decision. If anyone had managed to get someone to sabotage the boat, it was likely to be someone from the FNM, and the fact that they were holding a celebratory gathering made even more sense. She didn't think they were likely to admit it openly at the meeting, but someone might say something. She decided that she was going to go to the FNM gathering. Ideally, she'd like to take someone with her, but she certainly couldn't take Billy, he'd become an instant target, and she wasn't sure that Kate would approve. In fact, she knew that Kate would try and talk her out of it if she told her friend about her plans. Knowing that it would be hard to have brunch with Kate and keep it from her, Callie decided to resort to a little white lie and first thing, once Billie had hurried out to his football game, with a wave and a kiss and an "I'll call later", Callie sent her friend a text, crying off their regular brunch and suggesting that they meet Sunday instead. Kate replied that she was happy with that as she would have loads to tell Callie about her Saturday night date. Callie smiled to herself, her friend wouldn't be free to go out with her, even if she had asked. Much better to go alone, Callie thought. She would have a lot to tell Kate on Sunday as well, although she didn't imagine an FNM meeting was likely to lead to any romance.

Chapter 8

Looking through her wardrobe, Callie wondered exactly what one wore to an FNM meeting. Ringing her mother for advice wasn't exactly on the cards. She imagined the conversation:

"Hey Mum, what's the dress code for a fascist rally?"

"Definitely a dark colour, darling, a black shirt perhaps?"

No, ringing her mother was not a good idea. She decided on jeans, a plain white shirt and a blue jacket. Nothing flash. Nothing designer. She really didn't want to stand out in this crowd.

Even though the sun would be going down during the meeting, she decided on a pair of large sunglasses. She didn't want to be recognised by any of her patients, if they were there, or police, undercover or uniformed. And there was also the anxiety of being photographed and appearing in the morning papers. That would be very difficult to explain to her Asian boyfriend, no matter how tolerant he was.

There was also the anxiety over whether or not Lisa Furnow would be there. The fact that she dropped the flyer and was so flustered suggested she might be, but it could just have been something she picked up accidentally and was nothing to do with her.

Callie had argued with herself over whether or not she could befriend the crime scene photographer to try and find out her leanings, but it was well known that Callie was going out with Billy, so Lisa was never going to believe she was a member of the FNM and would be unlikely to confide in her if she was.

Callie wondered again about body number nine. Was he a member of FNM? Was it him who had sabotaged the boat? If so, it had back-fired spectacularly. She would have liked to ask Lisa if she recognised him, but the fact that the photographer hadn't come forward and identified the body, suggested not. That, or she wasn't prepared to admit to knowing him.

Callie's plan was to stay away from the limelight and do her best to go unnoticed, whilst taking note of the people and what they said. She hoped there would be talk that might link the group to the damaged boat. Something solid she could take to Miller. She would dearly love to see them prosecuted for murder, because if the immigrants drowned because of poor planning that would be manslaughter, but if the boat had been deliberately damaged with the intent that it would not be able to safely reach shore, that was unquestionably murder.

* * *

As she looked around her at the crowd that was rapidly gathering at the outdoor exhibition area on the seafront, known as The Stade, Callie realised she was still more smartly dressed than most of the other attendees. She smiled to herself, there was no time to change her clothes now, so she would have to do as she was.

She found herself a quiet spot between the gallery and the net sheds. She was slightly to one side of the main group, but she would still be able to hear the speakers who were standing on a makeshift stage comprising some piled-up wooden pallets.

With her sunglasses firmly in place as the sun set to the west, she was able to take a good look at the other people there. She recognised Peter Claybourne, the local councillor and amusement arcade owner, who had been so quick to say that no crime had been committed when a body washed up on the beach. How wrong he was. Callie wondered if he had known that at the time. Claybourne was talking to several people, shaking hands, but covering his mouth when he spoke, as if he was worried about others listening in, or lip-reading what he was saying. Perhaps the police were videoing the event, although, for her own reasons, Callie hoped not. Claybourne seemed to be telling the men around him something important, and Callie wanted to know what it was, but she dare not get any closer.

More people were steadily arriving and the area was becoming quite crowded. Callie edged carefully through the mass of people to get closer to Claybourne keeping a close eye out for anybody else she recognised as she did so. As the sunlight was slowly going, the evening was becoming cooler and her sunglasses more of a hindrance than a help, she took them off and stowed them in her handbag. She'd just have to hope no one recognised her.

The crowd was in high spirits and jostled her good-naturedly as she tried to move forward.

"What's the matter, love?" someone asked. "Go round the sides if you want to see better."

She waved acknowledgement and kept her head down. She had spotted Lisa Furnow quite near to her. She was wearing a hoodie covering her hair, and had a scarf around the lower part of her face, but that didn't stop Callie from recognising her – that was how she was used to seeing her in her crime scene coveralls and mask. Callie was saddened to have her suspicions about Lisa confirmed. The photographer was on the far side of Claybourne, not looking at him, but something about the way she was standing, still, intent, made Callie think that she was trying to listen in on Claybourne's conversation, just as Callie would have liked to.

Lisa looked up and saw Callie. Their eyes met for a moment, before both Callie and Lisa slid back into the crowd, each trying to pretend that they weren't there, that they hadn't seen each other.

As Callie regained her sheltered corner, out of the way and almost out of sight, there was the sound of someone tapping on the microphone at the front, and the crowd went quiet. All eyes turned to the front and Callie was surprised to see Darren Dixon climb up on the pallets and take the microphone from a burly man beside him. From the murmurs around her, others were also surprised to see Dixon. A chant of "Dazza, Dazza!" started somewhere and many of the crowd took it up.

"Evening all," he started and there was a roar of approval in response. "I'll bet you're surprised to see me, aren't ya? Just goes to show you can't keep a good man down. Well, you can't keep him behind bars when he ain't done nothing wrong, anyway."

There was another cheer and reluctantly Callie had to admire the way he was handling the crowd. The man was a pro, a natural, and he was enjoying every minute. She was surprised to find that he had charm and was even attractive in a rough diamond sort of way. No wonder so many women flocked to support him.

Dixon went on to talk about the tide of immigration and how everyone had to stand up for their rights and reclaim their jobs, and their country, from this foreign invasion. The sort of hate rhetoric that Callie despised and the crowd clearly loved.

Callie was more interested in the people listening to Dixon than the man himself, and she slowly scanned the crowd. She couldn't see Lisa Furnow anymore, perhaps she had decided to leave given that she had been spotted there. Callie knew that it was bound to cause a certain amount of awkwardness between them when they next met at a crime scene. Perhaps she ought to seek the investigator out before then, but what could she say? That she was only there because she wanted to see if she could find out if the FNM was behind the sabotage of the immigrants' boat? That she was spying on them? If Lisa was a committed member of the FNM she wasn't going to be pleased about what Callie was doing, and she was unlikely to be any help, either.

As she thought through the problem that this unlikely meeting might cause in the future, a new group of people – men and women, some young and some really quite elderly and carrying banners saying 'Anti-Racist League', and 'open borders now!' – had arrived. Callie could see that some of them even seemed to have young children with them, waving flags with peace symbols from their pushchairs. As Dixon began speaking again, the protestors started shouting, trying to drown out his rhetoric, much to the fury of some of his supporters.

"Murderer! Murderer!" came the chant, and it seemed to unsettle Dixon. He spoke to one of the men standing behind him and he nodded and disappeared into the crowd.

Some of Dixon's supporters were shouting and jeering at the anti-fascist groups, even shaking their fists at them, but they stood firm and continued their chanting.

"Murderer! Murderer!"

It was beginning to get ugly and as much as Callie understood why these people had come to disrupt the meeting, she wished they hadn't brought children with them. Or their grandparents.

Callie looked around, she could see a police van parked by the toilet block, and she hoped they were keeping a close eye on what was going on. She raised a hand and held it in front of her face, just in case it was too close an eye, and on film. Lisa was nowhere in sight, but

Claybourne was still standing there, listening to the speech and whistling his support of the FNM leader as Dixon moved on to the deaths of the immigrants and how they had brought it on themselves by raiding the country. Callie couldn't keep the disgust from her face, but then she saw David Morris pushing his way through the crowd towards Claybourne; he was not looking happy, in fact, he looked positively murderous. Sure enough, as soon as he got within striking distance of the councillor, that's exactly what he did. He threw a punch at the older man's head.

There was a shout and a scream and the two men disappeared from Callie's view, although from the movement of the men around the place where she had last seen them, they were kicking at something on the ground, and she suspected it was Morris rather than Claybourne.

As she pushed her way through the crowd, trying to reach the fighting men, Dixon quietened down, trying to see what was going on. Callie saw him signal to the last two men who were behind him, and in response, they began to make their way towards the disturbance, talking into their lapels, calling their colleagues to leave the generally non-violent anti-fascists and come and help with the real fight, no doubt.

"Looks like we've got some troublemakers here tonight, trying to give us a bad name. Don't let them ruin our celebrations." Dixon tried to stop things from escalating, but he was too late. Others among his supporters seemed to take the disturbance as a signal to turn on the protestors and scuffles seemed to break out everywhere.

Callie was getting close to Morris and Claybourne, or at least the spot where she had last seen them but she kept being shoved back by the people around her. She felt a prodigious shove in her back and she fell. Instinct made her curl up into a ball and shield her head from the flailing feet all around her. She tried to stand again, but the movement of the crowd made it impossible. There was more shouting and screaming and then: "Police! Let me through."

Callie was pushed back down, and she feared she was going to be crushed as people ran in all directions. Finally, the area around her began to clear a little and she was able to stand up, with a little help from Lisa Furnow.

"Thank you," she managed to say before the woman disappeared again.

Slowly, painfully, counting the bruises as she did so, she tried to walk and was satisfied that nothing had been broken. There were blue flashing lights appearing from all directions as police vans drove into the Stade area, each disgorging half a dozen uniformed policemen. They must have been waiting a short distance away to have got here so quickly and Callie couldn't have been happier to see them.

The crowd was dissipating fast at that point, and Callie saw Dixon being bundled off the pallet stage by his minder and pulled away to a waiting car. Going in the opposite direction to the majority of people, Callie still had difficulty pushing her way through and was almost carried along by the mass movement. With the judicious use of elbows and sheer force of will she finally made it through but by the time she got to Morris, he was unconscious on the ground, blood pouring from a wound to his head and Claybourne was nowhere in sight.

She knelt beside him as two policemen, helped by Jeffries who she was surprised to see, shielded her from the flow of people rapidly leaving the area.

Callie felt for obvious injuries to Morris's neck. Finding none, and concerned for his breathing, she rolled him gently into the recovery position, supporting his head as she did so.

"Ambulance is on its way, Doc," Jeffries informed her. "You okay?" He was looking at her chest.

She looked down and realised there was blood on her white shirt. She felt her head and quickly found a small cut and pressed a tissue to it. The bleeding seemed to have almost stopped, she was pleased to see.

"Fine," she reassured him. "It's nothing." She turned her attention back to the unconscious man, making sure he was breathing okay and slowly checking him for other injuries.

* * *

By the time Morris had been packed off to the hospital in the back of an ambulance, the cut on Callie's head had stopped bleeding completely and she had managed to clean herself up a bit with the help of some antiseptic wipes from the paramedic. She sat on the kerb and rolled her shoulders. She longed for a hot bath to ease the bruises that she knew she was going to have in the morning, but she had been told by the police officer who had taken her statement to wait, so that's what she did.

Most of the people had left the area once Dixon had been driven away by his minders. The police had detained one or two men but it seemed unlikely that anyone would be charged with anything. Callie's own statement said that Morris had thrown the first punch at Claybourne, and Callie didn't think that she would be able to identify any of the men who she was pretty sure had been kicking him once he was down on the ground. She couldn't even say for certain that they had been putting the boot in at all, she told the officer.

She took a long deep breath and closed her eyes. She would not be able to sleep, she was still slightly shaky from the adrenalin, but she thought a bit of breath control and a mindfulness exercise might help ease the tension.

"You okay?" Miller asked and her eyes shot open. That was all she needed, it had been bad enough to know that Jeffries was there, and that her activities were going to be the talk of the incident room, but this was way, way worse.

"Absolutely fine," she replied, levering herself up off the pavement. It hurt, but not as much as she had expected, she was relieved to find.

"What the bloody hell did you think you were doing?" he asked angrily.

"Trying to help a patient."

She stood on the kerb, pleased that she could look him almost in the eye with this advantage.

"I meant, what were you doing here?"

"I know, I know, I shouldn't interfere," she answered and hesitated, thinking about why she was there before replying to his question. "I wanted to see who was here, to see if anything was said that linked them to the boat sabotage."

"Didn't it occur to you that we would be here doing exactly that? Or that Darren Dixon" – Miller almost spat out his name – "would know that and be very careful that he said absolutely nothing that could be used against him?"

"Well, I didn't expect him to be that stupid, but I did hope that someone in amongst his supporters might be."

"And were they?"

"Not that I heard," she admitted. "But David Morris went straight over and laid into Peter Claybourne, continuing their argument from the beach. There has to be something going on there."

"Maybe Morris will tell us about it when he comes round."

"If he comes round," Callie corrected him. "We'll know more once he's been assessed in hospital."

Miller shot her a look.

"We will, not you. These people," he started. "Well, let's just say I'd feel happier if you didn't get involved."

Callie was pleased that he was showing concern, but she certainly wasn't going to admit it.

"David Morris is my patient, so I am involved."

"But that doesn't excuse you coming down here and getting in the way. We had it covered." His concern was replaced by anger.

"If that's all, I'll be going then," she said, and left with as much dignity as she could muster.

Chapter 9

Callie woke up on Sunday morning still aching from the night before. She groaned slightly as she shuffled to the bathroom. A hot shower helped her to get moving and she examined her bruises in the steamy mirror. They really weren't too bad, and not anywhere visible, so she had got off lightly.

The radio news was full of the near riot on Hastings seafront, as they described it. Callie thought it was more of a scuffle than a riot. There was only one person reported seriously injured and a few people had been treated with minor ones. Three people had been arrested, but Callie was sorry to hear that Dixon had not been one of them. In fact, there was a section of the report in which he told the journalist that the violence was nothing to do with his supporters, they were all angels, according to him. It was the anti-fascists, tree-huggers and anarchists that were to blame. They started it, apparently. Callie snorted in disgust and switched the radio off.

She made a quick call to the hospital. Once the sister in charge had checked she really was Morris's doctor, she told her that he had had a comfortable night.

"You can't be too careful, these journalists will try anything," the ward sister told her.

Callie agreed, and the sister continued to tell her that Morris was stable but not yet conscious.

A cup of tea, a bit of judicious make-up and a shirt that covered the small bruise on her shoulder, and she was ready for brunch with Kate.

The Land of Green Ginger was as welcoming as ever. Callie didn't like to think what it said about a person who felt more at home in a café than in their own home. The warm moist smell of tea, eggs and bacon made Callie want to audibly sigh with pleasure.

Unusually, Kate stayed quiet whilst her friend recounted the events of the night before.

"What the bloody hell were you thinking, Callie? You must know that those sorts of public meetings usually end up in a free for all!"

"I wanted to find out if they were involved in the boat sinking, that's all."

"What? You think they stuck a knife in it and sent the immigrants cheerfully on their way? Even they aren't that callous."

"I'm not so sure."

"And just how do you think they managed to do it?"

"They must have infiltrated the smugglers, had someone on board the boat they were on."

"A French boat? Can't see any of Dixon's mates speaking French."

"We don't know that it was a French boat. They could have transferred halfway across the channel. In fact, we don't know it was a fishing boat at all. It could have been anyone with a boat. There's a lot of money in people smuggling."

Kate had to concede that point.

"But what about your theory that the body at Fairlight was actually one of the smugglers? Do you think he would have got in the boat if he thought it was damaged?"

That was certainly a problem, Callie had to concede. Even she had to admit it didn't seem likely.

They both concentrated on their breakfast for a while.

"I read an article in the newspaper that it's often Eastern European gangs that organise it."

"Well, that's not going to make identifying his body any easier, is it?" Callie said, knowing she shouldn't snap at her friend. The fact was, she really wasn't looking forward to telling Billy all this later. Having Kate cross with her was one thing, but she was worried that Billy was going to be disappointed in her, which would be worse.

* * *

"Please tell me you won't go to events like that again," Billy said when she confessed, taking her hand and looking intently into her eyes.

"Well, I'll certainly try not to. It wasn't much fun and it wasn't very edifying, to say the least."

"You could have been seriously hurt."

"Yes, but I wasn't, Billy, and I'm sorry I've worried you, but I'm a big girl now and it's not like I could have taken you with me for protection."

"I could have been there with the anti-fascist bunch. Ready to wade in and fetch you out if there was any trouble."

She smiled at the thought.

"If I'd known they were going to turn up, I would have definitely suggested it, but you would have to have borrowed someone's toddler to do that, or take your granny along to fit in."

"Never!" he laughed. "My Granny could incite a riot in a nunnery."

He looked at her seriously again.

"It wasn't a very good idea, though was it? I mean, what if someone saw you there, or worse, you are in one of the press photos? It's not going to look good, is it? Local GP, and police doctor attends FNM rally?"

And he was right, she knew it. She just hoped that that there weren't any pictures out there. She could only imagine how angry Hugh Grantham, senior partner at her surgery, would be. Not to mention DI Miller. Or the Superintendent. She really ought to have thought it through. Losing her job, both jobs, was a very real possibility. She would check all the pictures on a variety of internet news sites later, she decided, although there was no way she could check them all, but at least she could reassure herself about the main ones.

"I promise I won't go to anything like that again," she agreed, and she meant it. It wasn't as if she had learned anything useful there, anyway.

Chapter 10

Monday morning, on her way to work, Callie bought a copy of the local paper and also a selection of the nationals. So far, there had been little coverage of the FNM rally in any of the major papers or the BBC and she sincerely hoped it would stay that way. Perhaps they had learned that it was best not to give divisive groups like them the publicity they craved, but she thought it was more likely to be because no one was that interested. There had been no deaths or serious injuries to report and not even a decent riot.

The local paper, however, was full of it, as you would expect, and when she had a moment, she quickly scanned all the pictures before breathing a sigh of relief. She couldn't be seen anywhere, not even in the wide-angle crowd shots.

There was a knock on the door and she quickly stuffed the paper in her bin as the practice nurse, Judy, poked her head around the door.

"Morning," she said. "Have you got a moment?"

Judy explained that it was her asthma clinic morning and that Anna Thompson had come in for review.

"She swears blind that she's using her preventers regularly and her peak flow is really quite good."

"But?"

"She's using an awful lot of salbutamol."

"Which she shouldn't need to if her preventer is working."

"Exactly."

"So, what do you think is going on? Do we need to try something different?" Callie asked her.

"No idea yet, but is it okay if I loan her a peak flow meter and ask her to keep a diary of her readings four times a day? I can get her back next week for review then."

"Of course, that sounds perfect," Callie answered, wondering why the nurse was asking her permission.

"Of course, she isn't keen to do it and she says she needs some more salbutamol to be going on with."

"Of course, she does." Callie sighed. "And what exactly happened to the last ones I prescribed?"

"She lost them, apparently."

Callie followed the nurse into the treatment room she used for her asthma clinics.

"Hi, Anna," Callie said to the young woman sitting in the patient's chair by the desk. "I hear you need some more salbutamol."

She was pretty underneath a thick layer of make-up, but even the pale pink lipstick couldn't conceal the resentful set of her mouth.

"That's right," the girl responded. "You have to give me more; else I'll have an attack. It's not my fault I lost the last one."

"Yes, of course. We wouldn't want you to have an attack, and I will give a prescription, but I just wanted to talk to you about it first."

Anna didn't look exactly thrilled at the thought of being on the receiving end of a lecture.

"We need to know why you are using so much because it might mean the type of preventer spray, the dark red one you are using, isn't strong enough."

"What do you mean? You're not going to change my meds, are you?" She looked anxious.

"Not if we can help it, but if it's not working, we may need to. That's why we are asking you to fill out the diary and come back to see the nurse next week. Then we can get a better picture of what's going on and if you need something stronger."

"Like what?"

"A course of tablets maybe." Callie turned to the computer and logged in to the girl's medication section. She did a prescription, despite the system warning her that Anna had already had several months' worth of treatment prescribed in the last few weeks.

"There," she said handing over the prescription. "But make sure you come back and see the nurse next week with your diary all filled out, and if you have a bad attack, or are worried, contact us, we can always sort out a nebuliser for home, if needs be."

Judy smiled and thanked Callie as she left, but the look the nurse gave her suggested that she didn't think it likely that Anna would be back the following week, and certainly not with her diary filled out. Callie thought she was probably right.

Once she got to her consulting room, Callie checked the girl's notes for something that told her about the family situation. A brief search on her address showed that there were six other patients registered there. Mother, grandmother and four children other than Anna, all younger than her. Callie could picture the houses at the address given and knew there couldn't be more than three or four bedrooms so it was bound to be a bit cramped with three generations living there. None of them were regular attenders apart from Anna and her grandmother who had high blood pressure and a heart condition.

As Anna was over sixteen, Callie couldn't enlist her family's help without her permission, and she wouldn't want to do that even if she could. Somehow, she had to make sure the girl was using her treatment properly and that she didn't need further help or stronger medication. If she was really using as much salbutamol as the prescribing history had recorded, there was a good chance she would end up in hospital in an acute attack, and also that the medicines the hospital would need to use would no longer work, because of the resistance to bronchodilators she must be building up.

* * *

Once she had finished morning surgery, Callie sat at her desk and procrastinated. She had shed-loads of paperwork to catch up on, but, having managed to put everything but her patients and their problems to the back of her mind for the duration of her surgery, she now couldn't stop thinking about seeing Lisa at the rally, and just what the subsequent fight between Morris and Claybourne was all about.

If she was ever going to get through all her work, she needed to try and find out what was going on so that she could concentrate.

First things first, she picked up the phone and called the lab, asking to speak to Lisa Furnow.

"She's not in today," the receptionist told her.

"Do you know when you are expecting her back? Only I have a query about one of the crime scenes." Callie pressed for more information.

"I can put you through to her supervisor if you like? I'm not sure when Lisa will be back, she phoned off sick this morning."

Callie declined the offer to be put through to Lisa's manager, as she really didn't know what she would say to them. She wondered if Lisa was really ill, or if it was something to do with having been seen by Callie at the

FNM rally. Maybe the crime scene photographer was worried that she would be reported for it, but that was ridiculous, because she could report Callie for exactly the same thing and attending the rally wasn't illegal. It might not win them many friends, but she couldn't see that it would be a sackable offence.

Callie picked up a prescription request and tried to forget about the rally but before she could settle back down to her paperwork, her phone rang.

"Hello, Dr Hughes speaking."

"It's me," Billy said. "Not sure if I should be telling you this under the circumstances, but body nine's routine blood tests came back. The tox screen is positive for cannabis, MDMA and ketamine. Oh, and a small amount of cocaine."

"What? That really is quite a mix."

"I know. And not exactly drugs you'd expect to find in an illegal immigrant, although some of the others have tested positive for cannabis, but not the others. Oh, and alcohol. He was over the legal limit for driving for that, too. Does that apply to driving boats?"

"Yes, being unfit to drive through drink or drugs applies to all modes of transport."

"I'm sending off some hair samples for analysis that might tell us if he was a long-term drug user."

"Surely Miller will have to realise that he doesn't fit with the others now."

"Yes, but look… I don't want you to go rushing in and—" He struggled to find the right words.

"Don't worry, I won't drop you in it with Miller." Callie was cross that he seriously thought she would get him into trouble.

"It's not that. I'm perfectly entitled to tell you the results and he probably knows I will. It's more that I worry about you going off and investigating things yourself."

Callie paused. It was nice that he was worried about her, she told herself, although a little bit of her resented it.

"I'm not going to go and investigate this, Billy. The only thing I'm going to do is go and give Miller a piece of my mind."

She could hear Billy giving a slight groan as she put down the phone, as if he wasn't sure that that was any better.

* * *

In an almost exact repeat of the reaction she got from Billy, Callie was sure that Miller groaned when he saw her walk into the incident room. The expression on his face certainly suggested that he had.

"Good afternoon," she said brightly.

"Doc," Jeffries acknowledged as she walked past him towards Miller's office. Everyone else seemed to look studiously at their computer screens.

"How can I help you, Dr Hughes?" Miller managed to smile and be polite as she came into the room.

"The tox screen on body nine?"

"You know what was found, then?" Miller shifted uncomfortably in his seat.

"Yes. And you can't tell me it was what you'd expect to find in the body of an illegal immigrant."

He looked as if he was going to disagree but Callie held up her hand to stop him.

"I know that drug use does happen, and particularly that drug use was rife in the Jungle, but since the French pulled that down and moved the refugees into more scattered groups, there has been much less." She wasn't exactly sure of this, but she was willing to bet that once the French police had broken up the gangs, drug use in the refugee encampments would have reduced, and that it probably wouldn't include such expensive and exotic drugs as had been found in body number nine.

"So I hear," he replied, clearly unconvinced.

"And the particular drugs found in body nine: ketamine, ecstasy and cocaine, would be even more unusual as they are more the drugs of choice for a more prosperous sort of person. Not a refugee who has just handed over his last cent, not to mention promised to work for nothing for the rest of his life to repay his debt in order to secure a place in a boat to England."

"What you are saying" – Miller spoke firmly, standing up and closing his office door so that the whole team weren't listening in – "is undeniably true, but it's not impossible that he is just another immigrant, or that he was a member of the gang supposed to deliver the group to their minders in England."

"In which case he might be known to Interpol."

Miller sighed.

"I promise you, Callie, we are looking into every possibility."

Unsurprisingly, he looked tired and Callie was reminded that not only was he dealing with probably the biggest case of his life, with the press and his senior officers breathing down his neck, but that he also had problems on the home front. She knew that Miller's wife had left him after some explicit photos had been sent to her. The pictures showed him tied up, in bondage gear, on a bed that was definitely not his own. The fact that he had been drugged and set up by a very clever woman, a serial killer he was investigating, hadn't mollified his wife. As far as Callie knew, she had yet to forgive him, let alone move back home.

"I'm sure you are doing all you can." She had to admit that, much as she might not always agree with the way Miller investigated crimes, or at least, where he put most effort, recent cases had proved to her that he did at least make sure all the bases were covered. "But I have a real feeling, belief, instinct, whatever, that this body doesn't fit with the others."

"Unfortunately, there is no real evidence to support that feeling."

"No evidence?" She almost shouted. "Apart from the fact that he was dosed up to the gills with expensive drugs, not to mention alcohol, you mean. He was definitely not sober, to the extent that if he wasn't one of the refugees, which would seem impossible, he couldn't be the smuggler in charge of the boat either. He wasn't in a fit state to steer a pedalo, let alone an overcrowded RIB in a storm. And" – she carried on despite Miller's attempts to interrupt – "and he had the tattoo of an English football club on his calf. It seems to me you have ample evidence that he doesn't belong with the others and that you need to investigate that probability straight away."

When she finally stopped, she was aware that everyone in the incident room was watching, and listening, to the argument. Miller glared at them, and they very quickly went back to their work.

"Look, I don't need you to tell me what I need to do or not do. And, frankly, it's more than a little insulting," Miller almost hissed. "I do know how to do my job, you know."

"I'm sorry. I'm just frustrated that no one seems to be listening to me."

"Perhaps if you spoke to them in a reasonable way, they'd be more likely to listen to you."

He really was cross with her, she realised. "I'm sorry. I'm sorry. You are absolutely right. I didn't mean to lose my temper like that."

"That's your problem. Running off half-cocked, interfering in things that have nothing to do with you. Like turning up at the rally on Saturday. What on earth was that all about? Didn't you realise we would be there, in the background, collecting information on everyone there?"

"Well, yes, I suppose I did," she said, although would she have gone herself if she really had known the police would be there? "But I wanted to find out if anyone knew anything about the sabotage to the boat."

"What do you know about that?"

"Nothing more than what was on the news. A journalist questioned the MP, Ted Savage, about it."

"Why did you think you might find out more at the rally?"

"Because it seemed like the sort of thing a fanatic from the FNM might do."

There were a few moments of silence. Miller seemed to be trying to make a decision.

"I can't think that anyone else would have any reason to damage the boat, can you?" she prodded him.

"The boat wasn't damaged, at least we don't think so," he finally said. "The lab has been over it very carefully, their report specifically raised the question of sabotage and then dismissed it. The damage all seems to be from the boat being dashed against the rocks. It's understandably hard to be sure but there are no cut marks that they can see."

"Then where did that reporter get the story?"

"That's exactly what we'd like to know. Unfortunately, he's fallen back on the old chestnut of needing to protect his sources."

Actually, Callie was all in favour of journalists being allowed to protect their sources. It was vital for whistle-blowers everywhere that they were protected but she could understand how frustrating it was for Miller in this case.

"Perhaps someone was trying to pin the blame on them?" she said finally.

Miller shrugged.

"Or it was just someone who wanted to give the reporter a story, you know, feel important for a moment."

"That's possible," she agreed, and it did have the ring of truth about it. "Why don't you make a statement to say that it's not true."

"What difference would it make?" he said, tiredness oozing from every pore. "People will still believe what they want to believe. Whatever the police say actually happened won't change a thing."

The trouble was, she knew he was right.

Chapter 11

Callie thought about what Miller had said about the person who had misinformed the reporter. He had said they might have been wanting to impress the reporter, perhaps even wanting a moment of fame. But, having given it more thought, Callie thought the timing of the leak, or fake news, was what was important. The interview had taken place just before the FNM rally and the news of the deliberate damage, wrong or not, was bound to stoke up feelings about it. Someone wanted to make the FNM seem either more villainous than they were, or more heroic, depending on your point of view. It was no wonder that the anti-racism groups turned up at The Stade in force, and no wonder it turned into the brawl that it did.

But who would want to do that? There was no doubt that Dixon and the FNM got plenty of publicity from both the report and the brawl, and all publicity is good publicity, or so they say, but was it? Would anyone honestly think that even being linked to the sabotage of a boat full of refugees who died was a good tactic? Even for an anti-immigration group, that was pretty hard-core.

So maybe someone wasn't trying to help them, but to break the rally up. Make sure the anti-fascists turned up in force, accusing the FNM of damaging the boat. Calling them murderers and making them look bad. Now that was an action that Callie could fully sympathise with, and the more she thought about it, the more she thought it might be what had really happened.

That said, who could have told the reporter, and, more importantly, would have been believed by him? It had to be someone who might really know. Newsmen were not complete idiots. If they were going to ask questions of an MP, they would want to be pretty sure the information was correct, or at least could be. And the fact that the source hadn't come forward openly suggested it was someone who might not be allowed to talk about it. Someone who the reporter would expect to have to shield. That is, someone from the police, the crime scene investigation team, or the lab itself, Callie thought to herself, as she poured herself half a glass of pinot grigio from the open bottle in her fridge. It was the last of the bottle and a brief inspection of her cupboards told her that there was no more. She was going to be sticking to health recommendations on drinking simply because not to do so would involve a trip to the shops or the pub.

Callie sat back down on her sofa and pulled her laptop towards her. She went to the website of the forensic lab. Lisa worked there and knew about the rally. The dropped flyer told Callie that, as well as the undeniable fact that she had been at the rally. And finally, Lisa was now off sick. Either she was embarrassed that Callie had seen her there and was worried that she would say something to her manager, or Lisa was hiding from other people. People who might be asking the same question that Callie was: who could have plausibly given false information to the reporter?

If Callie was right, that would mean that Lisa wasn't a member of the FNM and that, perhaps she had been trying to get them into more trouble or to disrupt the rally. Either way, Callie intended to get to the bottom of it. She just wasn't sure quite how, given that the CSI was not at work, as it meant she was going to have to find out where she lived. Or, at least, where she hung out.

A search online didn't give her any help there. Lisa's address wasn't listed in the phone book – so few people had landlines these days anyway – and Callie didn't know anyone at the lab well enough to ask them for it. She saw them all the time, of course, but that was professionally and besides, they were always covered in protective suits and masks. It was only because of Lisa's distinctive colouring that she was able to pick her out so easily, at crime scenes, but also in the crowd.

The reporter himself wasn't going to talk to Callie, but one of his rivals might. Callie went onto the local newspaper website. The bodies on the beach, the FNM rally and the brawl had given them many, many pages of material, not just reports on the events themselves but large numbers of editorial pieces, mostly written by one journalist, Debbie Smith. Helpfully, the website listed contact phone numbers and email addresses for its reporters in case anyone wanted to let them know about a story. Callie was pretty sure they would mostly get messages about parking, noisy neighbours and dog poo, but they might get the odd gem like when another body got washed up on the beach, and might even check the messages fairly regularly under the circumstances.

Callie picked up her phone and called the number. It was a landline so it wasn't surprising that she reached an answer phone.

"Oh, hi," Callie said once the message had finished, "my name is Dr Callie Hughes, I work for the police and wondered if there was any chance of meeting up?" Callie left her contact details and hung up. She had no worry that the reporter wouldn't get back to her as soon as she picked up the message. Journalists were always trying to speak to her about her role as a police doctor and get her to comment on local deaths. Callie thought that Debbie Smith would be more than a little eager to speak to her.

But, eager to get a response herself, Callie also sent an email, in case the reporter was in the habit of checking those from home.

Next, Callie called the hospital to check on David Morris; she was surprised to hear that he had been sent home.

"I didn't know he'd regained consciousness," Callie told the ward sister.

"Yes, he came round quite quickly. We'd have liked him to stay under observation a while longer but as he said there was someone at home to look after him and he was keen to go, we let him. I gave him a head injury information sheet, of course, and told him to come back if he experienced any symptoms from his concussion." The nurse was obviously keen to cover her back with her patient's GP, not realising that Callie wasn't really calling in that role. As far as she was aware, he lived alone, so she was surprised that he had told the ward sister that there was someone there to look after him. He must have been really keen to get out.

"Thank you for telling me, sister. I'll contact him and see if he needs a visit." Of course, generally speaking, GPs don't visit patients unless asked to do so, and often not even then, but Callie thought she could make an exception in this case. After all, it was only just gone seven in the evening, so she might just be calling in on her way home to check on him as the hospital had informed her that he had been discharged. She didn't need to tell him that she had contacted the hospital rather than vice versa.

* * *

There was a slight chill in the air as Callie walked along All Saints' Street. Morris's home was just off the narrow road, up one of the twittens that ran between All Saints' and Tackleway. These twittens, or narrow lanes, allowed foot access to cottages built on small bits of land sold off from people's gardens. Many of these homes dated back to the nineteenth century and were little more than two rooms with bathrooms added wherever they could be fitted in at a later time. The addresses of the houses in the twittens and their numbering were often eccentric and it always took new postmen, and new doctors, a while to find their way round. Callie hadn't been to this particular address before but she had been in many others nearby and was fairly confident she could find it from the lower road.

Finally standing in front of a door that had no number on it, but was in the right place to be number 15b, and which was in need of more than a lick of paint, Callie knocked.

"Yes?" a man called, before the door opened an inch or two and someone, a man, Callie thought, peered out.

"Mr Morris?" Callie asked. "It's Dr Hughes. Your doctor."

The door opened a little wider and Callie could see that it was indeed Morris.

"I didn't call a doctor."

"No, the hospital told me you had decided to go home and asked if I could visit to check you were okay."

It wasn't the exact truth, but it could be, Callie told herself as she put on her best concerned face.

"I'm fine," he said.

"I'm sure you think you are," Callie countered. "But if I could just run through the concussion tests, we'll all feel a lot more reassured."

He seemed to realise that she wasn't going to take no for an answer and stood back to let her in. It was a tight squeeze getting past him into the tiny living room that the door opened into.

"Sorry about the mess," he said. "I wasn't expecting visitors."

He wasn't joking, it looked like a bomb had gone off in the room leaving clothes, newspapers, takeaway cartons and empty beer cans littered around the place and all covered with a fine layer of cigarette ash.

Morris grabbed an overflowing ashtray and shoved it in the sink. He didn't have to move much in order to do it, the kitchen was just a corner of the room fitted with a mini cooker and fridge as well as the sink, which was full of water and dirty dishes, and now also had cigarette ends floating in there.

Callie tried not to show her disgust as she put her doctor's case on the floor and opened it, taking out an ophthalmoscope. Morris picked up a dark green packet of cigarettes that was lying on the table and chucked it into the kitchen. It was a bit late to try and cover up his smoking habit, Callie thought, as the evidence was all around him, hanging in the air.

"Right, if you could sit down, Mr Morris?"

He did as she asked and she looked in one eye, and then the other, flashing the light into them to check for a pupil reaction.

"You know the hospital only said you could go home because you told them there was someone here to look after you," Callie said.

"I hate hospitals."

"Yes, well, I can't say that I blame you, but that was a nasty knock on the head you got and we all need to be sure there's no lasting damage."

"I'm fine," he said again.

"Do you remember what happened?" she asked.

He shifted uncomfortably in his seat, and pulled some crumpled pizza boxes out from underneath his bottom. He chucked them in the general direction of the overflowing waste bin.

"Not clearly," he answered, hedging his bets. "The police say there was a scuffle between the FNM thugs and the anti-fascists and I got caught in the middle."

"Really?"

He had the good grace to blush slightly.

"You don't remember going up to Councillor Claybourne and throwing the first punch, then?"

"How do you know that was what happened?"

"I was there," she answered him. "A bit to one side, just watching in case anything kicked off," she hastily explained. "I saw it all."

"So, you saw those bastards putting the boot in when I was down."

"Yes, and I told the police that, but I couldn't see them clearly enough to identify any of them. They all had baseball caps and sunglasses on."

"Well, it was a sunny evening, wasn't it?" he said with a brittle laugh.

Callie moved some debris from the single chair next to the fold-down dining table, and gave it a quick brush with her hand before sitting down.

"What is it between you and Claybourne?" she asked gently. "I mean, you had a go at him on the beach, as well."

He looked up guiltily.

"It's not really something I can tell you," he finally answered. "Given that you work for the police."

"Okay, so can you tell me if it has something to do with the illegal immigrants who drowned?"

"No!" he shouted, looking horrified. "I wouldn't have anything to do with something like that."

"Well, that's good," she reassured him, although she was actually a bit disappointed to hear it. "You have to understand my asking, seeing as you were at that rally."

"I was only there because I knew he would be. 'course I hadn't really thought it through because if I had, I'd've known his goons would be there too."

"Is he connected to the FNM then?"

"Not that he'd admit it, but yeah."

"It certainly wasn't listed under his group memberships on the council website."

Morris smiled at that, and relaxed a little.

"And what about you?" she asked.

"Nah." He shook his head. "Not into politics. Claybourne says they're nicking our jobs, but I've never seen one of them on a fishing boat, so they're not the reason why I can't get work. It's them Spaniards taking all the fish, that's what it is."

Callie ignored the dig at the Spanish.

"So, what is your problem with him? Has Claybourne stopped you getting work?"

Morris shifted uncomfortably again.

"In a way."

Callie waited for him to expand on this answer, but it was clear he wasn't going to say any more.

"Did you know any of the men that laid into you?"

Again, Morris kept quiet.

"They could have killed you, David. You can't let them get away with it."

"I know!" He jumped up, angrily, and Callie shrank back, frightened at what he might do. Fortunately for her, he groaned and sat down again, gingerly rubbing his side.

"Cracked rib," he said by way of an explanation.

"That's going to hurt for quite a while."

"Yeah, so they said."

"Have you got any painkillers?" she asked him and he nodded at a half-full bottle of cheap brandy. Callie couldn't see a glass anywhere, so presumably he had been swigging it direct from the bottle.

"That's not a good idea. Not with a head injury." She rummaged around in her bag and brought out some painkillers. "These will be better for you."

He nodded and took them from her.

"Thanks."

"Look, I can't make you tell the police what's really going on, but I certainly recommend it," she told him. "Think about it. Please."

She stood and opened the door.

"Call 111 if you get any symptoms." She nodded in the direction of the hospital head injury information leaflet that she could see poking out from underneath the brandy bottle. "And make an appointment to see me later in the week. Or one of the other GPs, if you prefer."

And she left him, knowing that she had got nothing from him that was of any use, but at least hoping that he would take her advice with regards to alcohol and concussion. She had done her best as a doctor.

Chapter 12

Back at her home, Callie had made up her mind to call it a night and have a long relaxing bath. Whilst the bath was running, she checked her emails and saw that the reporter on the local paper, Debbie Smith, had got back to her and was keen to talk. She had left her mobile number and asked Callie to call her back whenever she could. She didn't go to bed early and would be happy to take a call, no matter how late.

Callie turned off the bath water, and picked up her phone.

"Hi," she said when the reporter picked up. "Callie Hughes here. Thank you for responding to my message so quickly."

"No, no, not at all."

As Callie had anticipated, the reporter was delighted to speak to her.

"How can I help? Has another body turned up?"

"No, nothing like that, thank goodness, although it is about the immigrants in a way." Callie hesitated, then decided, to go for it. "The story about the boat being deliberately damaged, I heard the television reporter ask

Ted Savage about it on the news, do you know where that story came from?"

There were a couple of seconds of silence from the other end.

"You want me to tell you who leaked it?" Smith queried.

"Not specifically. I understand how you might feel about not revealing sources. It's more that I want to know where the story first appeared. Who first said it had happened, publicly?"

There were a couple more seconds of silence.

"Are you suggesting that the story might not be true?"

The reporter was certainly quick on the uptake, Callie would have to be very careful what she said.

"I'm just trying to find out where and when the story started." Callie tried not to be explicit and hoped the reporter understood why.

"That's interesting," the reporter said, "because it caught us all on the hop. I've obviously tried to find out for myself. I've been in touch with all my usual contacts, but it didn't seem to come from anyone here in Hastings as far as I could tell, at least, that's what everyone is telling me."

"Not from the lab or the police then?"

"Not as far as I know, and certainly not from any of my sources. In fact, the first I, or anyone else here, heard anything about it was when the bloke asked Ted Savage the question. Obviously, I've tried to get confirmation everywhere, but I've come up against a brick wall."

"Where else could he have got the information?"

"Search me. I've drawn a complete blank."

"Is it possible that it came from the reporter himself?" she asked. "I mean, I'm sure he wouldn't…" Callie struggled to find the right words, she didn't want to upset anyone.

"Make something like that up? It's okay, it certainly happens."

Callie was relieved that she hadn't taken offence at the suggestion.

"It could also be that he was responding to a brief from his interviewee."

"How do you mean?"

"Well, sometimes when you are doing an interview and the person has a story they want to get out but don't want to be seen as the source, they tell you to ask them about it," she explained. "Ted Savage has form for doing that. He once got me to question him about a proposed change in fishing quotas that I knew nothing about. It was just a way to leak embargoed information, and whip up the outrage he knew it would cause, and all without getting into trouble. He's a good actor, too. Managed to look suitably outraged that I knew about such sensitive stuff when I asked the question."

"Did it work?"

"It did. The government backed down double quick when the opposition got wind of it."

Callie smiled to herself.

"So, if Ted Savage wanted to disrupt the FNM rally, without publicly speaking out against it, he could have deliberately planted that story," Callie clarified.

"I'm not saying that's what happened," Debbie quickly answered. "Although it's true he's always shied away from direct criticism of the group. I'm just saying that that could be the way it happened."

"Why wouldn't he speak out against them?"

"Because it's a marginal seat and he doesn't want to offend any possible voters. There's a fair amount of support for the FNM within the constituency."

"But he doesn't support them, either?"

"No, definitely not from what I know of him."

"So, he might try and disrupt things indirectly, you think?"

"Yes, particularly if the story wasn't true. Do you know if that's the case?"

"I don't know for sure," Callie responded. "I was just curious that no one had responded from the local police, to confirm or deny. It seemed strange to me."

"You and me both. And it's not for want of me asking, let me tell you."

Callie could believe that. She ended the call and added hot water to the now cool bath, knowing that she had probably set the cat amongst the pigeons. Debbie Smith was unlikely to let this drop now Callie had voiced her concerns. The question was, did it matter who had made the story up? Did it change anything? No one had broken the law, as far as she could tell; fake news was everywhere these days. But it made a difference to Callie in that she needed to know where Lisa stood. If Lisa hadn't been the source of the leak, then it looked likely that she supported Darren Dixon and his cronies and, much as it probably shouldn't, Callie admitted to herself that it would affect the way she worked with the photographer in the future, even after she had helped Callie when she was knocked down. It was bound to. And if she wanted to know for certain, she was going to have to ask either Lisa or the politician directly if they were the source of the story and hope they told her the truth.

As Lisa seemed to have disappeared for the time being, she had little choice but to try speak to Ted Savage. She just hoped that she managed to catch him before Debbie Smith did, although she thought that was unlikely. She was pretty sure the reporter would be trying to get hold of the politician first thing in the morning.

* * *

Next morning, Callie was unsurprised to hear that Lisa was still off sick, so there was no point in going to the lab and trying to speak to her. The morning was free from clinics and was allocated on her timetable for administration, learning and preparing for her annual appraisal. In reality, that meant she had time to try and track down her MP to ask him about that interview. She could always catch up with the other stuff in the evening.

Of course, tracking him down was easier said than done.

Ted Savage's website had contact details, but they only seemed to be for her to email him with any questions she might want to ask. He also held advice surgeries every Friday afternoon at an office on an industrial estate in nearby St Leonards and she could email or telephone for an appointment at that, outlining her problem beforehand so that his team could ensure he had time to research the answer. His Twitter feed and Facebook page had lots of comments on things, but nothing that would tell where he was likely to be at any given moment. She supposed that it was good security not to tell people where they could confront him.

She was fairly sure that he didn't live in Hastings itself but in one of the villages outside, and she remembered seeing him interviewed outside a house by the beach, but which beach was not something she could remember.

Of course, Debbie Smith was bound to know, but Callie wasn't sure she wanted to enlist the help of the reporter at this point. She had already given her a heads-up about the probable fake news.

Callie left a phone message, asking for an appointment at his next advice surgery, saying that she wanted to discuss the future role of police forensic physicians. She thought it sounded a reasonable request seeing as the role had changed and in some areas of the country, police doctors had been almost entirely replaced by specially trained nurses. She also suggested that they could meet earlier or at his convenience, but agreed to a surgery appointment if not.

With nothing more that she could do on that front, Callie decided to see if the police were getting anywhere with identifying body number nine as she thought of him.

It would be good if they actually had a name rather than just a number.

"Hi, Mike," she said when she finally got through to the coroner's officer. "I wondered if you had heard anything about the body found on Fairlight Beach? Body number nine?"

There was a pause before Parton answered.

"I wish there was, but it's going to be difficult identifying any of them."

"I fully understand that, Mike. I just thought this one might be easier, as it looks like he wasn't one of the refugees, what with the tattoos and the drugs and that."

"Well, the official view is still that he was one of them and that the tattoo and things could be because he had lived over here in the past. It's not uncommon for people who have been deported before to make their way back. Particularly if they have contacts or family over here."

Callie hadn't thought of that possibility and it certainly could explain the tattoo, if not the drugs.

"But if he's been deported already, wouldn't he be on a database somewhere?"

"Of course, and I'm sure that the police are checking them, but—"

"It's not a priority."

"Catching the people smugglers before any more die has to be their number one concern," Parton gently chided her.

"Of course, I know that. It's just that I can't help feeling that he doesn't belong with the others, not that he's more important than them, or anything like that."

"I know, but I can promise you, he hasn't been forgotten, and I, as well as the police, will be doing everything we can to identify all the bodies as quickly as possible. In fact, I think we do have an identification on one of the younger men. He's from Syria, sixteen years old and most of his family are dead, but he has an uncle who came over two years ago and has already been granted asylum. He was coming to join his only living relative."

"That's awful."

"Yes, it is. And I'm sure most of the others have similar stories. That's seventeen young men dead now."

"I'm sorry, Mike. I shouldn't be poking my nose in and disturbing you all when you have so much to do." Callie really did feel bad for interrupting him. After all, he had many more bodies that he needed to identify, every one of them somebody's son, brother or father, and every one a tragedy.

Callie needed to worry about doing her own job and stop trying to do others' work as well, she told herself firmly and settled back to an online tutorial regarding new guidelines for diagnosing dementia.

Chapter 13

Next morning, Callie got a message from the woman who was in charge of Ted Savage MP's diary. At least, that was the way she described herself. Callie was told that he could see her that afternoon, when he would be in his constituency office after a visit to a local primary school, or he could see her at his next advice surgery, the choice was hers. The woman made it clear that it was a very great honour to be given the choice and be allowed to decide for herself.

Callie checked her work schedule and accepted the appointment for that afternoon.

Before her own morning surgery, Callie checked the visit list and put her name beside a couple that she knew would be quick check-ins. Then she rang David Morris to make sure that he was still okay, and wasn't surprised that he didn't answer the phone. She left a message on his answer machine asking him to check in with the surgery, just so that she could be sure he didn't need another home visit, and then did a glance through the pile of prescription requests to make sure that Anna Thompson hadn't asked for any more asthma inhalers. It was a relief to find that she hadn't, so far.

After a deep breath to compose herself, Callie pressed the buzzer for her first patient of the day.

* * *

The MP's constituency office was on an industrial estate and nothing like Callie had been expecting. The parking area was rutted and had weeds growing up from cracks in the asphalt. There was only one car parked outside, a small flashy red hatchback. A quick glance through the windows showed that it was immaculate inside, as if it had been recently valeted. As if it was always recently valeted.

In contrast, the entrance to the office looked as if it had seen better days, like the carpark. Callie opened the door and went inside.

The woman in charge of the MP's diary turned out to be older than Callie expected. She looked to be in her early forties and was very conservatively dressed in a knee-length skirt and a flowery blouse done up almost to the neck.

"I'm Teresa Savage," she introduced herself, holding out a hand and making a quick grimace that could have been an attempt at a smile.

Callie was surprised and knew that her face had betrayed that fact. She knew that MPs had often employed members of their own family as a way of increasing the joint income from the taxpayer for work a spouse might well have done anyway, until the practice was banned. She dimly remembered that it was only banned for new MPs, suggesting that Ted Savage had already employed his wife and was allowed to continue. Callie's initial impression of Teresa Savage was of devoted secretary, not wife. Perhaps that's what she had been, before gaining promotion to the role of spouse, Callie thought. She certainly looked well-prepared to fight off the rude and belligerent constituents that no doubt made up a fair-sized proportion of those who attended advice surgeries.

Mrs Savage sat Callie in a bland, utilitarian waiting room, with uncomfortable chairs and a coffee table covered in advice leaflets, mainly about personal finance or how to claim various allowances and benefits. A picture of the smiling MP shaking hands with the last prime minister hung on the wall, alongside a portrait of the Queen.

Having refused the offer of tea or coffee, Callie settled down to wait and was pleasantly surprised that she didn't have to wait long. Too often, in Callie's experience, people with power liked to keep others waiting, just because they could.

"Dr Hughes?" Savage asked as he crossed the room, hand held out in readiness. He had a firm grip, but the shake was quick – not one to overdo the touching bit, she was relieved to find. Dressed more casually than he had been when being interviewed on the television, the MP was wearing a blue dress shirt, open at the neck, and cream chinos. His hair was greying at the sides and there were deep lines either side of his mouth but he still managed to look younger than the fifty-seven years his biography on Wikipedia had said he was.

He led her through to his office, a slightly better furnished room, with shelves full of files covering one wall. There was a table for him to sit behind rather than a desk, but a comfortable chair, unlike the two wooden dining chairs put out for those who came to see him. Callie was sure his offices in Westminster and at his home would be far more comfortable than this. His wife, she who was in charge of his diary, followed them in and at last it appeared that she could smile, if only for her husband.

"How can I help?" Savage asked once they were all seated and his wife had a notebook out and a pencil poised. To write down, what exactly? Every word they spoke? Perhaps she was there to note down any action points from the meeting. Or maybe she was just there for show, to impress Callie with how important a man Ted Savage was and how grateful she should be to be given some of his precious time. On the whole, she inclined to the latter view.

"I'm one of the forensic physicians for the area," she started. "We work with the police, and so have been closely involved with the recent deaths of refugees."

"Terrible, terrible." He shook his head. "Those poor young men. I can't tell you how bad I feel about it. Just dreadful. All they wanted was a better life, a place of safety, and look what happened. Such a tragedy," he said and Callie was impressed that he actually sounded so sincere.

"Yes, a tragedy indeed."

"In what way have you been involved with these poor young men, Dr Hughes?"

"I, and my colleagues, have been to each scene, where the bodies have been found, to formally pronounce death and try to form a view as to the nature of the death in order to direct the police investigation and the coroner in the right direction."

"Fascinating," he said and Callie was once again struck by the sincerity in his voice. "I assume it was fairly clear what had happened in all these cases, but it must be much harder at other times."

"That's true. Sometimes it's really not easy to decide whether a person died of natural causes or not, and we always err on the side of caution, suggest that the police investigate in case it is suspicious, but then the post-mortem may clarify things."

"Or not."

"Yes, sometimes even then we are not completely sure, but it's always easier to stop an unnecessary investigation than start one days or even weeks after the fact."

He nodded his understanding and leant forward.

"So how can I help you today, Dr Hughes?"

He looked at her expectantly, the formalities were over and he was all business.

"It was actually about the interview you gave last Saturday."

She was sure it wasn't just in her imagination that there was suddenly a slight tension in the air. Savage was sitting very still, smile fixed on his face, whilst Mrs Savage's back had stiffened and the knuckles holding her pencil were white. Callie worried that it might snap. Savage cleared his throat.

"Oh yes?"

"In the interview, the journalist asked about damage to the boat. I wondered if you knew where he had got the idea that anything like that had happened?"

"Goodness only knows." Savage waved a hand dismissively. He had recovered quickly, much faster than his wife. "Reporters seem to have sources everywhere and he's hardly going to tell me where he got hold of something like that, is he? Why do you ask?"

"Because of the timing of that interview and as a result, the question. You see, it's the first time that the possibility of sabotage seems to have been mentioned and it was the day of the FNM rally. It led directly to a counter-demonstration being set up by the anti-fascist and anti-racist groups."

Savage was unable to hide the look of contempt on his face when she mentioned the FNM.

"Can't say that I'm sorry that odious man had his rally disturbed. If I had my way, he wouldn't be allowed to hold them anywhere round here."

"Quite, but you can see why I'm interested."

Savage leant back in his comfortable chair and looked at her intently.

"Actually, I have to say that I can't see it. I mean, why would you be interested in finding out why an FNM meeting had been disrupted? Unless you were angry that it had spoilt their evening of gloating over the deaths and suffering."

She could feel her cheeks flush with anger at his suggestion that she might be an FNM supporter.

"I am not in the least bit upset that the rally was disrupted, although a man was injured and that might have been avoided, I am more interested in whose idea it was to drop that little bombshell into the interview guaranteeing that the disruption occurred."

Morris hadn't, of course, been injured by the scuffles that had broken out between factions, rather by his own attack on Claybourne, but she wasn't about to let the MP off the hook.

"I think there would have been a counter demonstration no matter what, but I agree it was probably larger as a result of the idea that someone had actively killed those young men by sabotaging the boat. Perhaps you should ask the journalist where he got the idea from."

"I have," she said. Although that also wasn't true, but the moment he suggested she do that, she was completely sure that he had indeed asked for the question to be added to the interview. In fact, she was pretty sure that the whole interview was set up, simply so that he could make sure of getting the idea out that someone, possibly from the FNM, had deliberately killed the refugees.

Callie looked him directly in the eye and saw that he knew that she was lying about speaking to the journalist, but he also understood from her look that she knew what he had done. A small smile played on his lips.

"Then you know that if he won't tell you, there's nothing you or I can do. I understand the information was false anyway. Perhaps he made it up to spice up the interview."

He glanced at his wife, who had managed to compose herself and immediately stood up. It was obviously a well-rehearsed signal.

"I'll see you out, Dr Hughes," she said and Callie found herself being ushered out of the office, with a smile and a dismissive wave from the MP, but at least she was sure now that the source of the fake news was the MP himself, and not Lisa. What she was going to do about it was another matter entirely.

Chapter 14

Callie whizzed through her visits and still had a spare hour before evening surgery. Deciding against calling in to see if there were any further patients she could help with, Callie walked down to the seafront. It was a lovely day and there were plenty of holiday makers taking advantage of the rare sunshine to have picnics on the beach. Callie bought an ice cream and strolled along with them, walking away from the pier and stopping outside the amusement arcade. There was a surprising number of people playing on the slot machines. By the ride-on toy car, a child was wailing and demanding to be allowed another go. His embarrassed parents were trying to reason with him and explain they had no more change, but he refused to be consoled until, spotting Callie's cone, the mother suggested an ice cream. That did the trick and the toddler raced along the pavement towards the ice cream seller.

Callie looked inside the arcade, which seemed quite dark in contrast to the bright sunshine outside, making it hard to see anything other than the brightly flashing machines. She was pretty sure that she couldn't see Councillor Claybourne in the place, but then, he was hardly likely to hang about in the arcade, or sit in the change booth. He probably had an office upstairs, or in the back of the building, or somewhere else entirely for all she knew.

She finished her ice cream and wandered round the room, checking to see if any of the penny drop machines, her personal favourites, looked ready to drop. The trouble was, they all did, that was part of their attraction, but she knew it was a lot harder to get money out of the machines than it looked. That was how the owners made their money, after all. Having made sure that Claybourne wasn't lurking anywhere, hiding behind the laughing policeman or one of the slot machines, Callie approached the change booth.

"Hiya," she said to the plump and pimply young girl sitting in there, looking bored. Callie expected a surly response from the girl.

"Can I help?" the young girl asked politely, making Callie kick herself, she must stop being so judgemental, she told herself.

"Is the owner in?" Callie asked.

"Mr Claybourne? No, sorry. He pops in, several times a day, to check on things, though."

"You don't know what time he's likely to be here next?"

"No, he likes to vary his routine," the girl explained. "Keeps us on our toes." She smiled, revealing twin train tracks of braces on her teeth. No wonder she didn't smile often.

Callie guessed Claybourne also liked to make sure no one was cheating him. She could see domes on the ceiling, suggesting CCTV coverage, not just of the change booth, but also dotted around the room. He would also vary the routine for dealing with the money collections, if he didn't want to get robbed. The sorts of businesses that relied so heavily on cash were easy prey, she knew.

Callie thanked the girl and headed back to work. She would have to find another way of getting to meet

Claybourne, hanging around the amusement arcade on the off-chance he visited didn't seem like a good use of her time.

* * *

Billy was working late, catching up with his normal workload now that the bodies had stopped washing up on the beach, so Callie was meeting Kate at their usual haunt, The Stag. It was music night and there was bluegrass in the back bar making conversation a little hard. As it was a warm evening, they decided to sit out in the garden where the music volume, not to mention the whooping and hollering of the music fans, was less, but ready to move back indoors if their peace was disturbed by flies, mosquitoes or particularly noisy children. They were discussing Callie's meeting with Ted Savage and her suspicion that he had primed the reporter in advance of his interview.

"It's sort of a variation on the lawyerly rule of 'never ask a question to which you don't know the answer'," Kate commented. She was wearing layers of linen, comfortably creased. Callie wished she could be that relaxed about her style.

"Yes, but one step further." Callie smoothed out an imagined crease in her skirt and picked at a bit of fluff.

"Exactly. If you have an answer you want to get out there, make sure you tell them what to ask. You have to admire him for it."

"Really?"

"Yes, he managed to do exactly what he wanted. He ramped up the protest movement by planting the idea that the deaths were a deliberate act of murder by the FNM, or whoever sabotaged the boat, and it disrupted their rally."

"And got Hastings even more bad press. Something it really doesn't need right now."

"*That* is also very true." Kate sipped her beer and stretched out her legs. "But at least it brought in some work for yours truly."

"What do you mean? Surely you aren't defending any of those people?"

"Why not? You wouldn't refuse them medical treatment, would you?"

"That's different."

"No, it isn't. Anyway, I can't afford to have principles, Callie. I have bills to pay and a few hours of legal aid work on a couple of affray charges that will probably be dropped for lack of evidence anyway, will do me nicely, thank you. And" – she did a little drum roll on the table – "I have a very nice case involving cigarette smuggling."

"I can't see that there's much money in a bloke bringing in a few extra packets, much as I'm pleased he got caught."

"This is more than just a few extra packets, let me tell you. This was a vanload of counterfeit smokes. And a big van at that. Not that he's admitting it's anything to do with him, of course."

"Counterfeit? You would think it was enough just to smuggle them in and avoid the tax."

"But if the cheap ones from goodness only knows where, have been made to look like genuine brands, they can be sold for an awful lot more profit. The EU decree that all cigarette packets should look the same and branding be removed has made it much easier for the fakers."

"Bet they didn't foresee that."

"Exactly."

"And they could have all sorts of dangerous chemicals in."

"I rather think all cigarettes do, don't they?"

"You know what I mean." Callie smiled despite herself, pleased to know that a vanload of harmful toxins had been kept off the streets and out of her patients' lungs. "I've heard stories of arsenic, mould and even asbestos in them."

"That's probably just to try and scare people off buying them." Kate was trying for dismissive but didn't seem overly confident in her words.

"I do hope you don't get this man off."

"Not much chance of that, not unless he decides to give the police the people who are actually behind it, or where they are distributing them and even then−"

"The CPS don't do deals."

"Not like they do in America, anyway, but it would at least help at sentencing to be able to show that he was cooperating."

"Where on earth do these counterfeit cigarettes come from, anyway?"

"I couldn't possibly comment, but Poland, Romania and Ukraine have been sources in the past, so I am told."

"Well, you have a pretty reliable source from what you've been telling me."

"If only I could get him to talk to the police."

* * *

Next day the local papers were full of news of the arrest of a man suspected of smuggling cigarettes. Thousands of cartons of counterfeit cigarettes had been found in the back of a van that had been the subject of a 'routine stop'. Callie smiled to herself, that was almost certainly code for a tip-off, she thought. Kate was right, it would keep her in work for months and the fake cigarettes were safely off the street.

There was a picture of a van, full of cardboard boxes presumably containing the confiscated cigarettes, and a larger picture of one of the packets displayed next to a skull and crossbones motif and a warning from Trading Standards that they could contain poisonous substances. The public would be able to tell if they had bought a packet, always supposing they didn't know full well that they were buying illegal cigarettes, because they were a darker green than they should be and the health warning was in an Eastern European script. Callie took a closer look at the picture; it looked suspiciously like the ones in the carton she had seen David Morris carrying the day she saw him coming out of the convenience store. Callie read the full text that went with the report. The packs were described as being a dark green, whereas real cigarettes all have to be in packs that are a regulation lighter, browner green colour.

Callie was the first to admit that she was no expert on makes of cigarettes, never having been a smoker, but as she tried to picture them in her mind, she was pretty sure she was right. The carton David was carrying that day definitely looked like the ones in the picture. He had been very quick to hide them behind his back when he saw her. She had thought at the time that it was because he didn't want his doctor to know he was smoking, but now she wasn't so sure. Perhaps he knew they were illegal.

Callie went back over her surprise visit to David's home as well. Had she seen any cigarettes then? There had been a packet that he'd chucked in the kitchen, out of her sight, and she was again sure that it had been dark green, just like in the report.

During her lunch break, Callie took a short walk to town and along the road to the shop where she had seen David Morris come out with the carton of cigarettes he was so keen to hide. It wasn't a shop she had ever been in before and it was hard to see inside because the door and windows were covered to stop exactly that. She knew that the shopkeeper would be able to see out even if she couldn't see in, so loitering outside wasn't an option. If she wanted to see what was inside, she had to go in.

At that moment, a man came out and, seeing her hovering by the door, held it open for her.

"Thank you," she said as she grasped the handle and went inside.

It was laid out much like every corner shop, with the counter by the door so that everyone would have to walk past it to leave the shop. There were cheap tins and packets of food crowding the shelves. Many of the labels were in foreign languages, and were for foods that Callie had never heard of, but more familiar British brands were there as well. Along with a large variety of alcohol, in bottles and cans, stacked at the back of the shop.

Aware that she was being watched by the woman behind the counter, Callie made for the chill cabinet and picked out a bottle of water. She hesitated over the ready-made sandwiches, before picking out a cheese and pickle one. She went to the till and put them on the counter. She could see a display case for cigarettes behind the assistant, but it was covered with brown paper so that she couldn't see the brands. For once, Callie was dismayed that the law meant she couldn't see the display.

"That all?" the woman asked in heavily accented English.

"Yes, erm, no. Do you sell cigarettes?" Callie could have kicked herself for asking such a foolish question, but she smiled and hoped the woman wouldn't think she was too stupid.

"What make?" the woman asked.

"What's the cheapest one you have?"

The woman gave her a look and reached into the cabinet behind her and slapped a packet down on the counter. It wasn't the dark green pack that she had seen with Morris or that was pictured in the paper, but the woman was already ringing up her purchases on the till, so Callie handed over a twenty-pound note and got little change in return. Either she had bought a very expensive cheese and pickle sandwich or smoking was a more expensive habit than she had realised. She hoped it was the latter as she chucked the unopened packet of cigarettes in a bin as she passed. She hesitated, then fished them out again; safer to dispose of them at home, she thought. Just in case a child found them in the bin and decided to try them out.

* * *

All afternoon, Callie dithered about what she should do about her suspicions that the shop she had visited was dealing in counterfeit cigarettes. For a start, it was just a suspicion, it wasn't like the shop had actually sold her one of the counterfeit packs.

Her first thought was that she should mention it to the police, but they had their hands full trying to track the people smugglers and with identifying the refugees. Another body had been found further along the coast and Callie sincerely hoped it would be the last.

She knew that she really should inform Trading Standards as they were the organisation who were investigating the scam, but then Kate wouldn't be able to persuade her client to tell them and help himself.

In the end, as Kate was busy in court, presumably defending her smuggler, Callie left her a message saying that she had information that the cigarettes were being sold from a particular shop and that she would hold off telling Trading Standards until the next day, to give Kate a chance to get her man to tell them first. Neatly getting round her lack of proof and helping her friend, all in one go.

She allowed a short moment of smug satisfaction at how she had handled it and a mental pat on the back.

Chapter 15

Callie was still feeling pleased with herself. Her plan to put pressure on Kate's client had worked and he had agreed to co-operate.

"They are going to raid the shop as soon as possible, but they were his only contact," Kate told her. "He wasn't able to help with who was organising it all, although he did say he didn't think it was actually the people who ran the shop who were in charge."

"Might be someone back in Eastern Europe, or wherever they came from," Callie said.

"Possibly, although he seemed to think that it was someone here in Hastings. Anyway, Trading Standards have promised to put in a good word for him if it all pans out, so hopefully he won't get too long a sentence."

"Maybe they should stake the place out, see if they can catch whoever is organising it."

"I don't think they have the manpower, and the police can't help, not with everything else that's going on and it's unlikely the person would actually go to the shop anyway, isn't it? They'd probably want to keep as much distance between themself and there as possible."

"True. I do realise that cigarette smuggling has got to take second place to people smuggling," she agreed, but something was niggling at Callie and she called the incident room after she had said goodbye to her friend and agreed to meet for Saturday brunch as usual.

"Er, hello, Dr Hughes," DC Nigel Nugent answered the phone.

"Hi, Nigel, quick question if you have a moment?"

"Of course. Is it about the identification of the bodies?"

"Well, yes, but also about the investigation of the people smugglers."

"Okay, what do you want to know?"

"Has there been any progress?" she asked.

"I've just finished touching up a photo of body nine, I've managed to make him look a bit less frightening."

"I thought Lisa, the crime scene photographer, was doing that for all of them."

"She touched them up to look clearer, but the subjects are still obviously dead and the Super said we couldn't release any of them to the public domain. I've photoshopped the eyes open and tried to make the face seem, well, alive."

He was clearly proud of his achievement and Callie had to admit, it must have been a pretty hard job to make the picture less likely to put people off their cornflakes.

"That's good, are you going to release it to the press?"

"I'm just waiting for the DI to agree to that."

"He will do, won't he?"

"I think so." Nugent seemed less sure. "I'll show it to him when he gets back."

"Back from where?"

"Calais. He's liaising with the French."

Callie realised that she shouldn't be surprised at that, everyone had assumed that the migrants had come over from there, either in the RIB the whole way, or brought part-way on a bigger boat; in either case, the French were involved.

"What about Sergeant Jeffries?"

"He's with DI Miller."

Callie's mind boggled a bit at the thought of Sergeant Jeffries in France.

"How long are they staying there?"

"I'm not sure."

"Well, couldn't you take it to the press liaison officer? Get her to approve it?"

There was a bit of umming and aahing from Nugent's end of the phone – he clearly didn't think he could.

"Or take it to the Superintendent? Get his agreement?"

"The thing is, Dr Hughes, he doesn't think it's a priority." Nugent was almost whispering and Callie could imagine him looking round the incident room, checking that no one was listening.

"You've already asked?"

"Sort of." Nugent was less than reassuring. "I told him I was getting the photo ready, but erm, well he told me not to waste my time on something that wasn't going to lead anywhere, because it's quite clearly just another boat person." This last bit came out in a rush and Callie could hear the anxiety and hurt in his voice.

Callie sighed, she knew she couldn't persuade the poor man to do anything about the photograph when the Superintendent had vetoed it, she would just have to wait until Miller got back and hope that she could persuade him.

"Okay. How about you send it to me?"

"Ooookay." Nugent sounded unsure. "No offence, Dr Hughes, but will you promise you won't release it before I have permission?"

"Absolutely, Nigel. I'll just use it to show a few people round here, see if anyone knows him."

She heard Nugent sigh with relief that she understood that he could get into a lot of trouble if she did release it, and she would never do that to him.

"Now to the other thing," she continued. "I take it there's no possible link between the people trafficking and the cigarette smuggling that Trading Standards are investigating?" Callie didn't want them barging into the middle of Miller's investigation and she wasn't convinced that they would have communicated with him about the planned raid.

As she had feared, Nugent knew nothing about it and promised to have a word with Sergeant Hales and make sure she was aware, but he confided that they were beginning to get leads on who was involved in bringing the refugees over by boat and that it didn't look as though it was a local gang.

"The working premise is that they were brought part-way over by a trawler, probably French and launched in the RIB from there," Nigel continued, confirming Callie's understanding of how they had been moved. "Coastguard tracking has possibly identified where they were launched, closer to Kent than here and for whatever reason, wind, tide, bad navigation, they ended up capsizing on our patch."

That was exactly what Callie wanted to hear. If it was just bad luck that the refugees had landed here, then the cigarette smuggling was unlikely to be connected. She thanked Nigel and hung up.

* * *

Callie was meeting Billy after evening surgery, they'd planned a quick drink and dinner at Porters, a local wine bar that was a favourite of Callie's. It had seen her through a number of disastrous relationships.

She arrived first, ordered a glass of wine for herself and a bottle of continental lager for Billy, before managing to find a table near the back. A light breeze through the open door kept the room comfortably cool.

Billy arrived not long after and she was able to tell him about the progress Nigel Nugent had told her about.

"Thing is, the picture he sent me is absolutely useless. He's stuck these open eyes on, that don't seem to quite fit, then smoothed over the cuts and bruises so that it looks like the poor man is wearing make-up. And then he's blurred it all to the extent that it could be pretty much anybody."

Billy laughed.

"Maybe you should get the lab to do it, they have all the equipment and could do a better job than a PC on a PC."

He was right, of course, but Callie didn't want to go into why she felt uncomfortable about approaching Lisa Furnow to do more work on the photographs she had taken of the dead. Not now. So she moved onto the news about Miller's trip to France and the theory that the migrants had been meant to land in Kent.

"Makes sense, not sure that anyone would deliberately send people to land on the beaches round here. The inshore fishing means they are more likely to be spotted apart from anything else."

Callie agreed. The beach-launched fishing fleet working out of Hastings was the biggest in the country, but further along the coast, towards Dungeness, there were a lot of quieter and safer places to land.

They went on to talk about the cigarette smuggling, Callie anxiously checking the tables around them, making sure no one could overhear, as she told Billy about the planned raid.

"I agree that it's great that they are about to close this bunch down, or at least that they will hopefully do that, but it's hard to get worked up about a few smuggled cigarettes when people are being treated in the same way – as a commodity."

"I know," Callie agreed with a sigh. "Although, we are talking pretty large sums of money being made from the cigarettes."

"And from the people smuggling. Not to mention that when they get over here, the migrants are indebted to the smugglers and often end up as modern-day slaves."

Callie knew he was right, and loved the fact that he cared so much. She stroked his hand.

"Let's hope they catch the people responsible for that as well."

Chapter 16

Monday morning, Callie felt rested and ready for whatever the week would bring after a rare weekend off. It didn't last long.

She arrived at the surgery to find that one of her colleagues had called in sick and Linda the practice manager was busy trying to cancel as many patients as possible and re-allocating the rest to the other doctors. Monday was never a good day for anyone to be off sick because they were quite busy enough already.

Callie could see that she had an extra two patients and a visit by her name, and what was worse, one of the appointments was for Mr Herring, a fussy little man who always had a great list of complaints, but rarely had anything actually wrong with him, at least, nothing wrong that wasn't actually of his own making.

Waiting for her in her paperwork pile was a prescription request for Anna Thompson; she needed more inhalers, urgently. Callie left a message for Anna to come in and see her, and, reluctantly, a prescription ready for the girl to collect.

Despite her heavier than usual workload, and the usual long discussion with Mr Herring, this time about whether or not he had a gluten intolerance, Callie was not running too late as she tackled her afternoon visits. Of course, she had only found the time to eat a sandwich in her car rather than take a proper lunch break, but as she drove away from the last visit of the afternoon, she realised that she was quite close to the forensic laboratory and on a whim, she went in and asked if Lisa Furnow was back from sick leave.

"She is," the receptionist told her. "Would you like me to let her know you are here?"

"Yes, please," Callie replied, although she was unsure if it was the right tactic. If Lisa didn't want to see her, it gave her ample time to nip out the back or just ask a colleague to say she had left for the day. On the other hand, Callie didn't really have much choice, she couldn't spend the rest of the day waiting in the car park for Lisa to come out.

To Callie's surprise, Lisa came down to reception.

"You wanted to see me?" she said as she approached Callie. She looked worried, as well she might, Callie thought. She'd used a liberal amount of make-up but the remnants of a black eye were still visible. The natural pallor of the young woman's skin meant that it was hard to miss, and must have been considerably worse in the first days after it happened. No wonder she had taken time off sick, it would have been hard to explain away.

"I wanted to thank you," Callie said. "For hauling me to my feet that night."

"It was nothing."

"Yes, it was, I could have been trampled."

"Is that it?" Lisa tucked a strand of her blond hair behind her ears, before remembering the black eye and looking embarrassed.

"Did you get that at the rally?" Callie asked.

"I need to get back." Lisa turned to leave.

Callie held out a copy of the photograph Nugent had emailed her to stop her going.

"I wanted to ask for your help," she said and gave Lisa what she hoped was a reassuring smile. "I needed a sanitised photograph of the man found on Fairlight Beach, so that I can take it round and see if anyone recognises him. That" – she pointed at the photograph in Lisa's hand – "is the best effort from the police."

Lisa examined the poorly touched-up photo.

"It's pretty crap," Lisa said.

"Yes, it's not very good, is it? I thought you could almost certainly do better."

"I should bloody well hope so."

"And would you do it for me?"

Lisa looked at her and hesitated before answering.

"Why are you trying to identify that particular body, Dr Hughes?"

Callie hesitated and Lisa led her over to some seats by the main door and they sat down.

"Because he doesn't fit."

Lisa said nothing, just sat, very still, and waited for Callie to expand on her explanation.

"He was the one found on Fairlight Beach, at a time when other bodies were being found further east. He was wearing clothes that could have been English in origin, and he had a tattoo of an English football club crest."

Again, Lisa said nothing.

"He was chock full of expensive drugs: cocaine, ketamine—"

Lisa looked up, surprised by that.

"I know that none of these things mean that he is English, that he isn't one of the migrants, necessarily, but it's enough, together, to make me want to be sure that he really is one of them, or at least, one of the people from the boat."

"You think he might be one of the smugglers?" Lisa asked.

Callie realised that she definitely had Lisa's interest with that.

"I don't know," Callie admitted. "That's my point. We can't know, definitively, not unless we find the proof, and at the moment, no one is looking. DI Miller is over in France, trying to find the traffickers. Mike Parton from the coroner's office is working with the incident team identifying the bodies, but they are working on the premise that they are all migrants.

"And what if this guy isn't?"

"Exactly."

"So, you think he's one of the traffickers?"

"Not necessarily." Callie hesitated. "What if he isn't from the boat?" For the first time, Callie actually voiced what she had felt could be true for some time. "What if he has nothing to do with this at all?"

"What? He just happened to drown on a beach right in the middle of a major incident like this, something that has never happened before? Bit of a coincidence, don't you think?"

"Or a deliberate act."

Lisa looked sceptical as well she might.

"Where better to hide a body than in plain sight," Callie explained.

"You think this man" – Lisa waved the picture at Callie – "was murdered and his body just added to the ones that were being found on a daily basis anyway?"

"Yes."

"Genius."

Callie looked at the photographer in surprise.

"You've got to admit, it is bloody clever, isn't it?" Lisa added.

"If I'm right and it is what happened, I suppose it is," Callie said. "I hadn't really thought about it like that."

Lisa was studying the picture intently.

"I'll go through my photos and see if there's a better one to tidy up. Do we know what colour his eyes are, because I'm betting they aren't bright blue like on here?" She waggled the photo Nugent had sent.

"I can find out for you," Callie said, then hesitated before adding, "Lisa, about, the um, rally? Did you get in a fight?" Callie indicated her black eye. "Did one of the FNM thugs, or the police…"

Lisa looked at the floor, her lips a tight line; she clearly wasn't going to say.

"It's none of my business, right?"

"That's right, Dr Hughes." Lisa stood abruptly. "It is none of your business."

Chapter 17

Callie was having a quiet moment between patients. A rare thing, and one to be savoured. She was leaning back in her chair, reading the local paper, drinking a mug of instant coffee and munching a plain chocolate digestive. What could be better? The news for a start, Callie thought.

The paper was full of the raid on a local shop where thousands of packets of counterfeit cigarettes should have been found. Unfortunately, none were. The shopkeepers were "helping with enquiries" but Callie was astounded, and embarrassed, that there had been nothing illegal to find in the shop. Had she been wrong? But then, it wasn't just her who had been wrong. The information hadn't actually come from her in the end, it had come from Kate's client, who was now not going to be able to use it to shorten his sentence.

Kate said he was as stunned as she had been when she heard. She assumed the mere fact of his arrest had caused the smugglers to change their distribution centre. Either that or they had heard about the raid somehow. Callie quickly went over her conversation with Billy in the restaurant, but she was sure no one had overheard. If they had got wind of the raid, it seemed more likely someone in the police let it slip. She sincerely hoped it was accidental rather than Claybourne having a source there, but she wouldn't put anything past him.

The article didn't mention any arrests other than the owner of the shop, though, and he would be out in no time if there was no evidence. Callie took another sip of coffee and thought about that. The police were now very much involved, which was a good thing, and they would hopefully put pressure on the shopkeeper as well as the van driver to tell them where the goods came from and who was the person behind it all. She finished her biscuit with a little sigh of pleasure and chucked the paper in the bin. Even if there was no evidence against the shopkeepers and the smugglers, they had, at the very least, been inconvenienced. With a bit of luck, they might even decide to cut their losses and stop smuggling cigarettes altogether. Or they might have to step up the operation to cover the losses. Either way, there was nothing more she could do, she'd done her bit to get the cigarettes off the market, and help Kate's client. She had to be satisfied with that.

It wasn't until later, when she was upstairs tackling her never-ending paperwork, that her day went even further downhill.

Anna Thompson had not turned up at the asthma clinic according to Judy, and David Morris had been admitted to hospital with serious injuries including several broken ribs and a ruptured spleen.

* * *

Despite it being her afternoon off, Callie felt she needed to do two visits before heading home. First stop was Anna Thompson's home.

If she had expected Anna to be at school, or for any of her siblings to be there for that matter, she was sadly mistaken. The whole family seemed to be running riot around the small terraced house. It was hard to count the younger ones as they never seemed to be still.

Anna, after a prod from her harassed mother, took Callie out into the garden.

"What's this about then?" she asked in a sulky tone.

"I think you know very well what this is about."

"I just need my puffers; else I can't breathe."

Callie took a deep breath herself.

"Look, I'm going to be straight with you, Anna. You're old enough to know the consequences of your actions. If you are really needing to use the blue inhaler that much, that means that your asthma is poorly controlled and you are likely to have a serious attack." Callie held up her hand to stop the girl from interrupting. "And if you do have a serious attack, then it's possible that all the treatments the hospital would normally use to try and stop that attack, would not work."

"What do you mean?"

Callie hadn't noticed that Anna's mother had come out into the garden and heard what she had said.

"I didn't think her asthma was bad?"

"It's not," Anna said. "So long as I get my inhalers."

Anna stood up, intent on avoiding any further conversation. Technically Callie should not continue talking about it now that her mother was present, but the damage was already done and she might as well be hanged for a sheep as a lamb.

"You are getting through far too many. We need to increase your preventer medication, maybe give you a course of steroids."

"I don't need that."

"Then I think we need to get you assessed at the hospital."

Anna looked sullen.

"Oh my God," her mother said. "Is it really that bad?"

"No, it isn't, Mum, the doctor's just making a fuss. Doesn't want me to have my inhalers, maybe they cost too much." She gave Callie a venomous look.

"The cost is nothing to do with it," she countered. "I am honestly worried as to why you are getting through so much medication. I spoke to the asthma nurse and she says your peak flows have been good, and she can't understand why you need your puffer so much. I think we need to do more tests and maybe refer you to the hospital."

"I don't want that."

"You'll do what the doctor tells you, young lady."

At least she had Anna's mother onside, although, as she left the house with Anna glaring at her, Callie wasn't sure if that was going to be enough to get her to attend an outpatient appointment, whenever that came through.

* * *

The second visit of the afternoon was to the hospital. She asked at the main reception and was told which ward had David Morris as a patient.

Speaking to the nurse at the desk, she was directed to the bay and could see him, drip in his arm, and a striped pyjama top, undone, revealed masses of bruising and a large dressing covering the left side of his abdomen.

If he was surprised to see her, he didn't show it. All the fight had gone out of him. Every ounce of his energy was being spent trying not to move and cause himself more pain.

Callie sat on the chair by his bed, as he eyed her warily.

"How are you feeling?" she asked.

"What's it look like?"

"Painful."

"Spot on."

"How did it happen?"

"I fell down the stairs." He couldn't look her in the eye when he said this and she knew he was lying.

"Really? Your injuries are more consistent with being beaten up. I'm even told that on your side there's the shape of a boot where you were stamped on."

"Must've landed on one of mine then."

Callie decided to change tack.

"The last two times I've seen you, you've been arguing with Councillor Claybourne. Why is that?"

"Let me see, maybe it's because the man's a prick."

"Why?"

"It's none of your business."

Callie was getting a little tired of being told this, not least because it was absolutely true.

"Look, David, I'm going to tell you what I think happened and rest assured, I have absolutely no proof for any of this. I think you and Mr Claybourne had a falling out about the cigarette smuggling, and that when the shop was raided, he blamed you and had you beaten up. If that's the case, I'm sorry, because it was me who told Trading Standards about the place and I'll happily tell him so if that's what you want, but I'm not sure how much help that would be."

Morris stared at her, open-mouthed. Of course, it wasn't strictly true that she had told Trading Standards about the shop, she had merely threatened to, thereby forcing Kate's van driver to tell them.

"How did you know about it?" Morris managed eventually.

"I saw you coming out of the shop with a carton of cigarettes that matched the description of the smuggled ones. So, I suppose, Claybourne could argue that you were the source of the information, but it wasn't deliberate and I will leave your name out of it. I have to warn you, though, that I am also going to tell the police about my suspicion that he is behind it."

"No, please don't, Dr Hughes, please don't go to the police." Morris was understandably frightened at the prospect.

"I'm sorry, but I have to. I will also suggest that they might need to offer you some kind of protection and I think you should agree to co-operate fully with them, because you don't want to give Claybourne the chance to come after you, again."

She left Morris to consider what he should do next, and she had a word with the ward sister on her way out.

"I'm worried about my patient in Bay C," she said. "I think he may try and discharge himself, and there is also the possibility that the men who beat him up could come back."

She left the nurse rapidly making arrangements for a member of security to come up to the ward. Not to stop Morris from leaving, that was his right – although Callie didn't think he was in any kind of a state to leave hospital just yet – but to stop anyone else from having a go at him whilst he was still there. At least she felt that she had done all she could to protect him – whilst he remained in hospital, anyway.

* * *

Having had a thoroughly unsatisfactory afternoon, Callie decided to round it off with a visit to the incident room to see if DI Miller was back from France. He was. And so was Detective Sergeant Jeffries.

"Hiya, Doc. Or should I say bonjour?"

His accent was execrable, but Callie was impressed that he had at least attempted to learn one French word.

"How was your trip?"

"Fantastique!"

She was wrong, he'd learnt two words.

Callie was lucky that Miller came out of his office before she had to listen to Jeffries telling her more than a few choice phrases about French ladies and their sexiness, and how they had all apparently loved his accent. Callie found it hard to believe and the faces of his colleagues in the incident room told her that he had been telling them all about it, at length, ever since he had got back.

"Sounds like you had an interesting trip."

Miller's mouth twitched as he tried not to smile at her choice of words.

"That's one way of putting it." He led the way over to the refreshment station which was situated beside two boards at the front of the incident room. Callie paused to look at the photographs that completely covered one of the boards. One picture for every victim found. Normally there would be details of the victims written beside their photos, but only one had even a tentative name next to it – the young lad that Parton had mentioned, Callie presumed.

The pictures were all clearly of bodies, hard enough for relatives and friends to see and not suitable for the general public. Whilst she had been visiting Morris in the hospital, Callie had been sent the touched-up photograph that she had requested from Lisa Furnow. There was no doubt it was a much better option. Whilst there was still something about it that suggested that the man in the picture was not alive, he wasn't so obviously dead and there remained enough detail for him to be recognisable to people who knew him; his friends, and his family.

"I've emailed a better picture of the body found at Fairlight over to you," she told Miller. "So that you can try and identify him, maybe put it in the papers."

Miller grunted and looked distracted.

"Where the hell?" he asked and looked around.

The refreshment station was never more than a table with a kettle and a coffee machine as well as an array of mugs, packs of teabags, jars of coffee. Only, at the moment, the coffee machine was empty apart from a ring of sediment at the bottom of the pot, there were no mugs to be seen and only a few crumbs and an empty packet remained of the supermarket own-brand custard creams. Miller sighed, but at that moment DC Nugent hurried over with a tray of clean mugs and the kettle.

"Sorry, Guv. Just cleaning up a little."

"You are a star, Nigel," Callie said and tried not to smile as the young man blushed.

"Not at all, Dr Hughes. My pleasure." He hurried away and whilst the kettle boiled, Callie set about making tea for herself, and Miller put two spoons of coffee into a mug.

"The photo?" she prompted.

"I'll check it out."

She was going to have to be satisfied with that. For now.

"Was it useful, going to Calais?" she asked him.

"Yes," he answered. "And no. There's no great will over there to stop the migrants from crossing the Channel."

"That's understandable, from their point of view."

"I know. Much easier if they become our problem rather than theirs, but they did at least promise to follow up on our leads."

"That a trawler brought them most of the way over?"

He nodded and stirred his coffee. Callie sniffed the milk carton. Miller didn't take milk, she knew, and she wasn't sure she wanted to trust it, but it smelled all right so she poured a small amount in her tea.

"Using the coastguard radar, we managed to track all the fishing boats on the night in question. They all have to have these identifying transponders and they have to leave them on at all times, but in one case, the marker seemed to disappear for a short while."

"They could have been coming closer to shore, dropping the migrants off in a RIB and then switched it back on once they were back where they should be."

"Exactly."

"Have they been questioned?"

"That's where we have to leave it to the French, and they have promised to follow up."

"But they may not follow it up too vigorously."

"To be fair to them, they don't like the people traffickers any more than we do. I think they will take it further, it's just that they'll do it in their own way."

"And in their own time. Meanwhile, the traffickers could be getting ready to bring another boatload across."

Miller shook his head.

"I made it quite clear that we had the boat's registration number and if they come anywhere near our waters, we'll intercept them with a naval vessel. Make an international incident out of it."

Callie smiled. She would like to see the Royal Navy stop them in the act.

"I read in the paper that there were to be more patrols."

He nodded.

"Anyway, is there anything we can do for you, Callie, or is this just a social visit?"

"Has Nigel told you about the cigarette smuggling?"

"I seem to remember reading a memo. Didn't Trading Standards raid a shop or something?"

So, she told him about everything that had happened, Morris's two spats with Councillor Claybourne, seeing Morris with the cigarettes, telling Kate about which shop he had bought them in, leading to the abortive raid and finally, that Morris had been badly beaten up.

"So, let me get this straight. You think Claybourne is the man behind the cigarette smuggling and that he suspects Morris grassed him up?"

"Yes."

"And do you have any evidence of any of this?"

She had to admit it was a good question.

"Not really. Just that I witnessed Morris having a go at Claybourne twice, and definitely coming off the worst at the rally. It stands to reason when he turns up in hospital for a second time, that it's Claybourne behind it again."

"I agree that there is some circumstantial evidence there to suggest it, but not enough for me to go charging in asking Claybourne awkward questions."

"Seeing as he's a councillor, and all," Jeffries said.

Callie could have done without him coming over and butting in.

"It's big business, bringing in tobacco. Lots of money involved," she continued. "If Claybourne is running a smuggling operation, it stands to reason that he would want to protect it. His treatment of Morris shows he's prepared to resort to violence, and body number nine, really doesn't belong on that board there." She pointed to where the photographs of the dead migrants were.

Jeffries gave an exaggerated sigh.

"Wait. You think he's part of the cigarette smuggling ring rather than the people smuggling?"

"It has to be possible, hasn't it?"

"Bloody hell, Doc, now you're accusing a councillor of bumping people off."

"Is that so hard to believe?"

Both Miller and Jeffries gave it some thought.

"You have to admit that it seems unlikely." This was the best that Miller was prepared to say.

"Like a three-legged horse winning the Derby," Jeffries added as he shook the empty biscuit packet. "Who's nicked all the custard creams?" he asked belligerently. "Bloody thieving bastards."

Chapter 18

Another mild summer's evening, another body washed up on Fairlight Beach, and Callie was once again wishing that it wasn't in quite such a remote place as she stumbled for the umpteenth time, slipping on the wet rocks. When she finally got to the spot, a bit further along from where body number nine had been found, Callie saw that this was the body of a young woman. The only female so far and that was not the only reason to believe that she was not one of the migrants: she looked Caucasian, with badly bleached hair dyed purple at the ends, a couple of piercings to her nose and eyebrow; and she was dressed in cheap but fashionable clothes. And she had a serious head wound.

Lisa was busy taking photographs while her colleagues, all masked and dressed like Callie in their crime scene overalls, were searching the area around for anything that might relate to this body.

"Who found her?" Callie asked Lisa.

"Same bloke as found the last one. I think he's probably going to give up being a detectorist."

Callie thought she probably would too, if she had found two bodies in less than two weeks.

"Thanks for the photo, by the way, it's really good."

"No problem." The photographer looked over Callie's shoulder and then turned away. Callie looked round and saw two more suited and booted people walking along the beach in towards her, neither had their masks pulled up yet. Miller and Jeffries. As she watched, Jeffries slipped on a wet, algae-covered boulder and landed on his rump. She could hear him swearing from where she was and she turned away, trying not to laugh. It was hardly appropriate at the scene of a violent death.

"What you got for us?" Jeffries asked gruffly as he pulled up his mask, attempting to deflect from his embarrassing entrance. Miller had already raised his mask and was looking at the body. He turned to listen to her answer.

"Body of a young woman, not been in the water long, hard to say if drowning or the head injury are the cause of death, but—"

"Definitely not one of the boat people?"

"Not unless she's been living somewhere nearby for the last couple of weeks, no. They might know more after the post-mortem."

Miller looked up at the cliffs above the beach.

"Could she have fallen?"

Seeing his gaze, Lisa started taking photographs of the area above them. The steep cliff was topped with dense woodland, but Callie knew from her walks that there was a path, sometimes steep, sometimes muddy, winding through the trees. It had once gone all the way from the East Cliff of Hastings to Fairlight Cove, but landslides in some places meant that a few sections were now missing or too dangerous to use.

"Anything's possible," Callie answered him. "But she's lying a bit far out for a fall."

"Could have fallen at high tide, been washed out and back in again."

Jeffries had a point, but they all knew that could mean she fell in from almost anywhere.

"Colin?" Miller called, and Colin Brewer, the crime scene manager, recognisable in his protective clothing by his short, squat stature, hurried over. Miller pointed up the cliff. "We're going to need a team to walk along the top of the cliff, see if she fell from somewhere up there."

"I'll get a team ready for first thing in the morning, Guv."

Miller looked as if he was about to argue and ask for them to start the search straight away.

"Don't want any of them falling over the cliffs in the dark."

There was only about one hour of daylight left, Callie knew, and it would take longer than that to get a team of searchers together.

Reluctantly, Miller nodded his agreement.

"What about this body and the tide?" he asked the crime scene manager.

"We should be able to clear the beach before it comes in," Brewer reassured him. "If we hustle. The difficult bit will be getting the body back to where the van is parked before we get cut off. Need to get moving soon."

"Bloody hell," Jeffries commented as the little man bustled away to make sure his team had collected as much of the surrounding detritus as possible. "Not exactly a convenient place to find a body."

And Callie had to agree.

* * *

Billy was in his office when Callie popped in at lunchtime the next day. She had been called to the hospital to take swabs from a young woman who had reported that she had been raped. Callie found sexual crimes particularly difficult and after an hour of collecting evidence and counselling the distraught young woman, felt she needed a break before returning to do her evening surgery.

"Hiya," Billy said, but Callie couldn't help noticing that his smile and greeting were not as cheerful as usual.

She sat down in the chair opposite his desk and gave him a long look.

"What's up?"

"If you've come to ask me about the young woman found on the beach last night, the body has already gone so that the Home Office pathologist can do the PM in better facilities."

"Ah," she said and understood. Callie's godfather had been the local pathologist until his death and over the years, she had listened to his frequent complaints about Home Office pathologists coming in and taking over all the interesting cases.

"Have you thought about registering to be one yourself?" she asked.

"Of course, but it's not that easy."

She raised a questioning eyebrow.

"Nothing worth having ever is," she quoted her mother's favourite phrase from when she was growing up and complaining about having to work so hard to get her A-levels.

"It's not just the qualifications, I have completed quite a few of the modules already and I'm working my way towards the rest," he admitted.

Callie tried not to look surprised, or hurt, that it was news to her.

"It's more that you have to be a member of a recognised group practice and there's only six of those in the country."

Callie understood his concerns.

"The ones that come here always seem to come from South London."

"That's right, there's a large practice covering the whole of the south east. It makes it easier for the rota to make sure that there's always someone on call."

"And what are the barriers to joining them once you do have the qualifications?"

"Firstly, they'd have to have a vacancy and they don't have one at the moment. In fact, they have a waiting list."

"And secondly?"

"If I joined them, most of the work would be in London, which is understandable. I'm not sure living down here would make sense."

He looked at her and she could see his problem. When he was living and working in Brighton, the roads were faster and covering London would have been less of a problem. He might even have considered moving up there anyway, as his family were from a suburb to the south of the city. But the roads and trains from Hastings made commuting to London difficult and the town hospital was a small one, lacking facilities – a backwater for the career-minded. If he wanted to be a Home Office forensic pathologist, or at some point he decided to turn to teaching, become a professor even, he would have to move. He would have to leave Hastings.

It was a dilemma she understood well. She had watched her godfather struggle with it over the years and had often thought that he regretted staying in Hastings. Work versus home life was a delicate balance, as she knew only too well, and you had to be happy with the way it worked for you.

"If you want to be a Home Office forensic pathologist, Billy, you have to go for it. We'll work something out, but I'll never hold you back."

He came over to her and gave her a hug.

"Thank you," he said and smiled, only this time he looked like he meant it.

Callie just wished she could ignore the knot of anxiety that had formed in her stomach.

Chapter 19

The evening news had included a short item featuring pictures of both body number nine and the young woman found the day before and asking for information about them. They had used the picture that Lisa produced for Callie, which made her happy that she had braved her concerns about meeting the photographer again after the rally, and set her wondering again about the black eye she had tried so hard to cover up. Callie was sure she must have got it at the rally, the question was, who was responsible? It wasn't surprising that Lisa had decided to take time off work because of it – a crime lab was the last place you could get away with saying you walked into a cupboard door, they spent far too much time analysing evidence in domestic violence cases to let that go.

"About time they started to try and find out who body nine really was," Callie said crossly to Kate.

"Better late than never," Kate replied, opening a packet of crisps and laying it on the table between them. "The pictures were very clear, I can't believe no one will recognise them."

"I know. There will probably be hundreds of calls." Callie knew that Miller had been given a team of civilians on overtime to answer the phones in anticipation. She just hoped they were able to pick out the ones with real information from the time wasters that always responded to appeals for information. They were often well-meaning souls, calling to claim their long-lost son or daughter, who would be in their fifties by now so it couldn't possibly be them, or just to say they were praying for the poor young things, but not realising that all they were doing was clogging up the lines and stopping the police from listening to the people who really could help.

It was Friday night and The Stag was heaving. It was hard to talk over the noise of people drinking to celebrate the start of the weekend. Even the garden was packed, so they squeezed into a corner, next to a family of weekenders. The two small children were clearly bored and kept jumping up and down, knocking the table and spilling their drinks. Callie and Kate didn't usually come to The Stag on a Friday because it could get too busy. But pretty much every pub in town was busy on a Friday night.

"Do they think she was dumped at sea, like the bloke?"

"Seems that way. The police checked the cliff above, but there was no sign she had been up there and jumped or was pushed, although it's not easy to be sure."

"Are there many places you could throw yourself from along the clifftop?"

"Not really, it's not like Beachy Head along there. The paths are generally further inland and it's heavily wooded most of the way, so you would most likely get caught on a tree or bush. Why, are you thinking of pushing someone off?" Callie couldn't imagine Kate killing herself, someone else was much more likely.

"Always handy to know. In case."

"You could always take a walk along the cliffs and check it out for yourself."

"Get real." Kate laughed. Callie knew that walking was her least favourite form of exercise.

There were a few moments' silence and Callie's mind drifted back to Billy and her worry about their future.

"Come on, tell me about it or I'll have to resort to torture, or buying you another drink," Kate said with a concerned smile.

"Tell you what?"

"Whatever it is that you are fretting about."

"Is it that obvious?"

"Yes. Apart from everything else, you usually go out with Billy on a Friday, or rather, stay in with him."

Callie hesitated, Kate was her best friend, and there was little she had kept from her over the years, but somehow her concerns about their future seemed too close and personal for friendly chat just yet. That, and she didn't know where to start.

"It's nothing, he's busy working, that's all." Callie didn't think she had fooled her friend for a moment, their friendship was too long and too close for that, but she hoped she hadn't offended her by holding back.

"Please tell me you haven't split up."

"No! Nothing like that."

"Good, and I'll accept that for now," Kate told her, "but just make sure you come to me if you need to talk it through with someone."

"I will, I promise," Callie replied. "But for now, I think I need to be patient and see how it pans out. I might be worrying about nothing." But her voice belied her concerns. What would she do if Billy moved away? Up sticks and follow him? Or stay and try to maintain a long-distance relationship. That might be possible if he took a post in London, but what if there were no vacancies as he had said and he decided to look further afield? The North? Or even to go abroad? Could she, would she, want to leave Hastings?

Kate was watching her closely as all these thoughts went through her head.

"I think another drink is called for," she said and grabbed their glasses.

She was right, but Callie also knew that if she had a few more she might open up and tell all her worries to her friend. Perhaps that's what Kate was hoping, and who knows? Callie thought, perhaps that would be the best thing.

* * *

Next morning, it was a beautiful clear day and Callie decided to walk to work. She had a slightly muzzy head from all the alcohol she had ended up drinking the night before. She had indeed ended up telling her friend all her worries after a couple more glasses of wine, and Kate had been her usual robust self, telling her to stop worrying about something that might never happen. After all, she had argued, Billy could fail his exams.

As if, Callie had told her, Billy had never failed an exam in his life. So, giving up that line of argument, Kate had concentrated on the likelihood of a vacancy coming up with the London practice of pathologists and Billy getting it. They giggled as they discussed ways of creating a vacancy and whittling down the competition. Callie favoured a mass poisoning whilst Kate suggested a sexual scandal of some sort.

Even with all these scenarios being nothing more than fantasy, discussing it had made Callie feel better. She knew she needed to put her worries to one side and give Billy the space to decide what he wanted for his future, and if that involved leaving her behind, so be it. She would survive. She was surprised that overnight, whilst she slept, she seemed to have made the decision that even if he moved away from Hastings, she wouldn't. Perhaps that told her something deep and meaningful about their relationship, or at least her relationship with the town and the people who lived there. She honestly didn't know why she felt that way and now wasn't the time to try and work it out, she thought. Not with a hangover.

As Callie reached the bottom of the East Hill steps, she could see David Morris, sitting on a wall. His face was badly bruised and he had a grey tinge that told her, even from a distance, that he was in pain.

"David! What are you doing here? Have you discharged yourself from hospital again?"

He grunted as he tried to stand up, before deciding to stay as he was.

"I wanted to tell you something, before going away to, um, convalesce," he explained.

Callie had to admit that leaving town made sense, Hastings certainly wasn't a healthy place for him to be at the moment.

"Have you told the police where you are going?" she asked, knowing that they were the last people he would have spoken to. "Or who did this to you?"

"No." He grunted again and shifted his position slightly in an attempt to get more comfortable, he clearly didn't want to talk about being beaten up. "To both."

"But if you talk to them, tell them what Claybourne's up to, he'll be arrested and you will be safe."

"Safe?" he snorted in derision. "I'll more likely be dead."

Given how badly he'd already been beaten up, Callie wasn't about to argue with him on that score. She knew that even if Claybourne was arrested, he would almost certainly get bail and go after Morris again, unless the police put him in protective custody, and that wasn't likely to happen.

"I used to drive them over for him, but I got pissed one time and missed the ferry and he got a replacement."

"The cigarette smuggling?"

He nodded.

"I just wanted back in, you know? But the bastard wouldn't let me. Said I was too unreliable."

Callie couldn't argue with Claybourne on that, with Morris's drinking problem he could hardly be called reliable.

"Was it you who told the police about the van? Got the new driver arrested?"

He nodded again.

"He guessed it was me. Threatened my mum. She's in a home, for Christ's sake. Doesn't even know what day it is. That's why I went to the rally and, well…"

He shrugged. She knew the rest.

"So, why did you want to speak to me?" she asked. "Just to tell me you were leaving?"

"No. It was about that picture they showed on the news," he said, "the girl."

"Did you recognise her?" Callie couldn't disguise her interest.

He nodded.

"She was going round, asking questions."

"About what?"

"Her boyfriend. Said he'd gone missing."

"Do you think he could have been the man in the second picture?"

"Maybe. I didn't really look at the photo she was showing everyone." He gave her an apologetic look.

"Where was she asking about him?"

"I was in the club and she came in." Callie knew he meant the Fishermen's Institute and Social Club in All Saints' Street, a favourite haunt of Morris's because the drinks were cheap there.

"Do you know anything more about her? Where she was from? Was she alone? How long had her boyfriend been missing?" Callie could hardly contain herself, she had so many questions.

"Whoa!" He shook his head. "Like I said, I didn't talk to her myself. Sorry. She did say she was down from London – I know that. But, you know, I didn't speak to her and no one in the club said they'd seen him, so she left."

Despite her continued questioning, he had nothing more to add and after a while, levered himself off the wall.

"Thanks for telling me this, David."

"Yeah well, I could hardly tell the cops myself, could I?" he said with a smile. "Got to be going now."

She watched as he walked, slowly and carefully, up the road towards the Old Town. She hoped he'd be all right and she wished he would tell her more about Claybourne's operation, and just how far he would be prepared to go to protect it, but after a quick look at her watch she hurried on down Rock-a-Nore Road to the new surgery premises. She was going to be late if she didn't get a move on.

* * *

Before Callie was able to even start her morning surgery, she was called into the police station to see a prisoner who they wanted to interview and needed to be sure she was sober enough. There was a mad scramble as Callie tried to see as many patients who were already waiting as possible, and Linda, the practice manager, worked to re-allocate or cancel others before she could leave. The result was that she had no time to call the incident room and tell them of her conversation with David Morris. Instead, she resolved to speak to them when she had finished with the prisoner.

Once at the station, she found out she had been called to see Marcy, again. A regular both in the cells and in the surgery, Marcy was a drug user and prostitute who had been known to assault her customers on more than one occasion, whether that was the service they had asked for or not. Callie had tried to get her into rehabilitation many times, but Marcy just didn't seem interested.

"What am I going to do with you, Marcy?" Callie asked having checked her over and found her relatively sober, and with nothing more than a few minor cuts and bruises.

She had been arrested for being drunk and disorderly in the early hours of the morning. Unfortunately, she'd bitten a police officer during the arrest, so there were going to be greater charges added in, and on which the police, and CPS, were still deciding. Resisting arrest and assaulting a police officer for certain, and they could go all the way up to attempted murder, depending on circumstances. Police officers generally didn't like to be bitten by drug addicts, for obvious reasons.

"Messed up again, didn't I, Doc?" Marcy replied, apparently unperturbed by the fact.

"Yes, you did. Now, are you going to let me take blood to check for hepatitis, HIV and any other blood-borne diseases, or am I going to have to get a court order?"

Marcy held out her arm by way of reply. She knew the drill, which was a relief for Callie, and for the officer involved, as ruling out any nasty diseases would at least give them some peace of mind, provided Marcy tested negative, of course. The custody sergeant had told her the officer in question had already been sent to the hospital for his own blood tests and to have the wound cleaned up, and Callie knew he would also be offered preventative medication whilst they awaited the results, just in case Marcy had infected him with anything.

"Why did you do it, Marcy? Think of that poor officer and his family."

Marcy hung her head in shame and didn't even flinch as Callie took the blood sample.

"Sometimes, I just lose it, you know?" she explained.

"You need to get yourself sorted out, Marcy, once and for all."

"Easier said than done, Doc." Marcy hesitated. "I don't suppose you can give me something? I'm going to be here a while, I reckon."

Callie wrote her up for some methadone to see her through and left her, looking resigned to her fate. Optimists would say that if she was sent to prison it would be her opportunity to get clean, but Callie knew that wasn't the case. Drugs were just as readily available inside as they were on the street.

Feeling thoroughly depressed, Callie walked up the stairs to the incident room so she could tell them her information about the girl in person.

There was a buzz of excitement in the room that told Callie something had happened, and glancing over at the whiteboard, she saw a tentative name next to the dead girl's photograph: Michelle Carlisle.

DC Nugent bustled up to the whiteboard as she watched and stuck another photograph next to the first. It showed a younger Michelle, pouting for a selfie. It was undoubtedly the same girl and Callie was both happy that they had identified her, and sad for the family that would now know that she was dead.

Callie intercepted the detective as he returned to his desk.

"What do we know about her, Nigel?" she asked him.

"Hello, Dr Hughes." He blushed as he spoke. "Michelle Carlisle was eighteen, family home in Bolton. She was reported missing three years ago after she apparently ran away to London with a friend. The friend came back a few weeks later, but Michelle chose to stay. The family say there's been nothing heard of her since."

"Same old story," Jeffries said from just behind her, making her jump. "Preferred selling herself on the streets to being rogered for free by her stepdad at home."

He was right, it wasn't an uncommon story, but it was still a sad one.

"Nothing on the man?" she asked, knowing that if there had been any news, it would have been written on the board.

"Still checking out a few possible leads," Nugent said. "But none of them are looking promising."

"Which might suggest he was one of the traffickers and nothing to do with the girl."

Callie turned to Miller who had come out of his office to join in the conversation.

"Except that she was looking for him." That certainly got their attention.

"What?"

"I bumped into a patient this morning who told me that she had been showing a picture of a man around, asking if anyone had seen him. Said he was from London." She petered out as Miller seemed to be going quite red in the face.

"If you could come into my office, Dr Hughes, I'd like to hear the details. Now!"

He turned on his heel and walked into his office. Callie could feel every eye in the room on her as she hesitated. On the one hand, he had no right to speak to her like that, particularly in front of a room full of colleagues, but on the other hand, she had information she wanted him to have as quickly as possible. She also wanted to convey it in a way that didn't land David Morris in even more trouble than he was in already. She followed him and as he sat behind his desk, chose to stand opposite him. Needless to say, Jeffries had followed her in and closed the door behind him.

"Why haven't you told us this before?" Miller demanded.

"Because it only happened this morning, on my way to work," she responded, tight-lipped and furious with him for being so unnecessarily rude.

Miller wiped his face with his hands and she could see how tired he was, and she relented, sitting down in the visitor chair. He really did seem angry and Callie wondered if perhaps he had just told his senior officer that he didn't think the two were connected and would now have to change his report. Maybe she should have found the time to speak to him before.

"I came in as soon as I could, but got waylaid by the custody sergeant. So here I am, telling you now."

"And what exactly are you telling us?"

"This man, my patient, said that the girl in the photograph, Michelle Carlisle, was in the Fishermen's Club showing round a photograph of a man and asking if anyone had seen him. She claimed he was her boyfriend and he was missing."

"And the photo she was showing round was of the man we know as body nine?"

"He doesn't know. He didn't look at the picture, but it's a bit of a coincidence, isn't it?"

"And he's sure it was her?"

"Absolutely."

"We'll need to speak to him. Confirm it all."

Callie hesitated; this is where it got difficult.

"This is a murder enquiry," he reminded her.

"I'm perfectly well aware of that," she snapped back. "It was David Morris."

"I thought he was in hospital?" Jeffries said.

"He discharged himself."

Jeffries headed for the door.

"Right, Jayne, Dick, move your arses, we're going to pick up David Morris." Jeffries grabbed a jacket and headed to the incident room door, followed by Jayne and another DC.

Callie decided to keep quiet about Morris's plans to leave the area. They'd find that out soon enough and there was no need for her to admit she knew what he was going to do. It would only make matters worse.

Chapter 20

"Have you come in to say 'I told you so'?" Mike Parton said when Callie walked into the mortuary hoping to see if Billy was free for a late lunch.

"I told you so," Callie responded with a smile.

"Told you so what?" Billy asked them both.

"That body number nine wasn't anything to do with the migrant boat," Callie said.

"Well…"

Mike wasn't prepared to go as far as that, clearly.

"We know he wasn't likely to be one of the migrants, that's all. He still might have been one of the smugglers," he said.

"Then he would have been French, or whatever nationality they were, surely?" Callie wasn't prepared to let her theory go so easily. "The girl looking for him was from London."

"What girl?" Billy was lost in this conversation.

"The girl who was showing his photo around town."

"A photo of a missing boyfriend, possibly body nine, and then she wound up dead," Mike explained to the bemused pathologist before turning to Callie. "One of the ladies at the club has confirmed what you told Miller, and she is pretty sure it was a photo of him."

Callie was relieved for David Morris. She knew that he wouldn't have been in when Jeffries went round to his home, and was unlikely to return there in the near future, but now that the police had confirmation of what he had told her, it would be less urgent for them to find him. Although, she knew, they would probably still like to talk to him about Councillor Claybourne and the cigarettes, not to mention to ask him who had beaten him up.

"Right, so they were connected, the girl whose body was found and the man, body nine?" Billy was trying to sort out what this meant.

"Which is why I came down to see you," Mike explained.

"Of course." It was all becoming clear to him, but Billy did not look pleased. "He will need another PM, done by the Home Office pathologist."

"I'm sorry, it's just in case they are connected."

"It's not your fault, Mike, it's the rules. It's just irritating."

"I'm sure they won't find anything you've missed."

"So am I." Billy was very sure of himself, he knew he was a very thorough and very good pathologist. "It's the waste of time and money involved in redoing it that gets me."

Both Parton and Callie knew that wasn't strictly true. Autopsies were often done more than once, for the prosecution and the defence, in complex legal cases. It was a way of making sure that nothing was missed, although in practice, it often introduced an element of doubt, because two doctors would rarely agree completely.

Billy went to his office door and called out for his technician, who quickly appeared.

"You'll need to get body nine ready to transport up to London or Brighton or wherever the Home Office pathologist says he wants it, Jim. Now, if you don't mind, I have work to do."

Billy went into the changing room and closed the door, conversation over.

Jim looked at Parton and Callie and shrugged before disappearing back into the storeroom.

"I don't think he was best pleased," Parton said.

"No," Callie agreed.

"Maybe he should think about getting registered with the Home Office himself," Parton said.

"He is," Callie said.

"Ah."

Nothing else needed to be said.

* * *

"I'm sorry," Billy said later in bed.

"About what?"

"About snapping at you and Mike in the mortuary."

"Oh that, I thought you were apologising about your performance."

He sat up.

"Are you saying I need to apologise for my bedroom skills?"

"No." She laughed. "You certainly do not."

They kissed, and then he lay back, serious once again.

"I was cross about them re-doing the PM on body nine and I really wasn't looking forward to the job I had to do that afternoon, but that's no excuse for taking it out on the two of you. Or Jim. He had to help with it as well, and he didn't shout at anyone."

"I don't remember you shouting, just prancing off and slamming doors."

"Prancing off? You make me sound like a schoolgirl." He shook his head and lay back, remembering his afternoon.

"What was it?" Callie asked. "The job that you weren't looking forward to?"

"A schoolgirl. Sixteen. Only she won't be prancing off anywhere and slamming doors. You think I'd be used to it by now."

"What was the cause of death?"

"Asthma attack, according to the ED consultant, and I couldn't disagree, she had hyper-inflated lungs and mucous plugs grossly restricting the airways. Apparently, she was completely unresponsive to treatment, he said. There was nothing they could do, so sad."

Callie sat up, suddenly panicking.

"Her name wasn't Anna Thompson, was it?"

Billy hesitated as he thought for a moment.

"No. I'm sure it wasn't. It was Colleen or something like that. Why?"

Callie relaxed.

"Patient," she explained. "Over-using salbutamol. I warned her of exactly this when I saw her last."

"Well, go round and warn her again. I tell you, I don't want to see another young girl in my mortuary for something so preventable ever again."

Callie would do exactly that, she decided. She had to make sure Anna understood the possible consequences of her actions, if she wouldn't reduce the over-use of her inhaled medication, Callie would have no choice but to change her to a non-aerosol treatment. Callie felt it was important that she understood that, so she would put a clear plan in writing for the girl, with exactly what course of action Callie would take if she didn't comply.

Before she fell asleep, another thought occurred to Callie: she should talk to Mike Parton and get him to check if there had been any other cases in neighbouring areas. Perhaps there was a trend for young girls to misuse their asthma medication. If so, it needed to be raised with the coroner, and advice sent out to GPs. As Billy so rightly said, no one wanted to see any more dead young girls.

Chapter 21

Mike Parton's office was tiny, but so neat that Callie often wondered if he used a ruler to make sure all the reminders on the pinboard were equally spaced.

Parton hurried back into the room with two mugs of tea before she had a chance to move something just to see if he noticed.

"I was going to talk to you about that," he said when she explained her concerns about the young girl who had died from an acute asthma attack. "When I spoke to the consultant, he said there had been another two girls admitted recently in a similar state, but that they had been able to save them both; bit touch and go with one though."

"Three? That's not normal."

"No, and they were all from the same school, so I wondered if we should get someone in to speak to them all, teachers and pupils, try and nip whatever is going on in the bud."

"That sounds like a very good idea. Do you have any idea why it's happening? What does the coroner think?"

"He seems inclined to believe it's just a coincidence and there won't be anymore, but I'm not so sure."

They both knew that small groups of diseases often occurred naturally and did not necessarily mean that there was a common cause. Those not well-versed in the laws of probability would always lean towards there being a reason for groups of occurrences and it was often hard to persuade them that these clusters did happen randomly.

"Except that I also have a patient I'm concerned about as well and I think it's always best to err on the side of caution. I'll have a chat with the lead asthma consultant, I don't think I'll have any problems getting him onside. If you want to let the head teacher know, I'll give her a call, see what I can sort out."

"Thanks, Callie."

They sipped their tea in silence for a moment before Callie asked about the investigation into Michelle Carlisle's death and body nine.

"I know the police have had multiple confirmations that she was looking for our man, but they seem no closer to identifying him from the missing person databases."

"Are they still working on the assumption that he came over with the migrants though?"

"No, I think they have accepted he's from the UK, but might still have been here to collect the migrants, picked them up in the boat and then they all got into trouble."

"Seems unlikely."

"I agree, but their problem is the sheer number of people being reported missing every year, and we have no reason to assume he went missing recently."

"He could have gone missing years ago? As a young boy, or teenager maybe?"

"Exactly," Parton said. "He may have changed a lot over the years he's been away, new tattoos will be no use to identify him with now. The police are going back through the registers, but the number of potential matches is huge."

"Can't they doctor the photo, make him younger somehow? Maybe someone would recognise him as a young boy."

"It's possible, but even with the new age regression software it takes an expert to get a good likeness, it's not like social media where it doesn't matter if it's nothing like you."

"Are you saying it's expensive?"

"Yes." Parton nodded.

"But it might be better than nothing."

"True. And it's something to think about if they don't find him. In my opinion, they will probably get there, but it could take months to narrow it down."

Callie knew he was right, but that didn't make her feel any better.

"Meanwhile, we are no closer to knowing what happened."

* * *

When she spoke to DS Jayne Hales on the phone later, Callie heard that Miller had gone to London to liaise with the police there, and see if they could find out where Michelle had been living in the years since she had run away from home, and more importantly, who her friends were. They were hoping to find someone who might recognise her boyfriend – body number nine.

"More likely to get to his identity there than here. We've had no one ring in and say they recognise him on the helpline, well, no one credible that is, so it doesn't look like he was from round this neck of the woods."

That left Callie wondering why he had come to Hastings and what had he done to get himself killed. If he was the English contact for the people smugglers, why was he in the boat with them? Surely, he would have been on shore, with a van or lorry, ready to transport them elsewhere once they had landed. She said as much to Jayne.

"We haven't found any evidence that they were being met this end so far," she told Callie. "We are checking all the ANPR cameras to see if perhaps they were being met further up the coast in Kent, which would fit with the theory that they turned up in Hastings because they'd got swept along by the tide."

"Are you still working on the premise that he was part of the smuggling operation?" Callie asked.

"The Guv thinks it would be too much of a coincidence if he wasn't."

Callie disagreed about that, but DS Hales was not the person to complain to, she'd save it for when she next saw Miller.

"What about the girl?"

"Well, clearly she wasn't on the boat, because she was found so much later," Jayne conceded. "And she didn't drown. Dead before she went in the water."

"You've had the PM report back already?"

"No, just a brief phone call with that news."

"So, what's the theory?" Callie couldn't hide her interest. "Had she fallen or been pushed off the cliff then?"

"Well—" The policewoman hesitated. "No, they don't think so. She had no injuries apart from the ones to the head which killed her and the pathologist said there would be more if she had reached the beach that way. Plus, she had definitely been in the sea, so the working theory is that she was dumped overboard from a boat."

"Like her boyfriend."

"Yes."

"It can't be from the same boat if he came in with the migrants because you have that boat, well, what's left of it, anyway."

"Exactly. We're checking the movement of every fishing and leisure boat along the coast in the forty-eight hours before she was found, as that would cover the probable time of death."

Callie finally let the sergeant go, she had a lot of work to do, after all, tracking down all the trawlers and yachts that had been out and about that night. But what if the boat didn't have its transponder switched on, like the boat that dropped off the migrants? Callie knew it was a risk that the coastguard might be sent out to check on them under those circumstances, but if they were not out for long, they might have been able to get there and back, and that was always supposing she had been dumped from a boat big enough to have a transponder. If it was just a small RIB or tender, meant for inshore use, it wouldn't have one at all.

Callie just had to hope that they were able to track even small boats on the coastguard radar and might be able to see where the boat had come from, if that was the case, but she wasn't sure that they would.

* * *

Friday, with the promise of a weekend off to look forward to, plus seeing Billy that night and plans to meet Kate at some point, meant that Callie was in a particularly good mood. As she walked towards her consulting room, the last person she had expected to see in the waiting room was Lisa Furnow. Callie was pretty sure she wasn't even a patient at the practice.

Lisa stood as she saw Callie, so she had been clearly waiting to see her and not anyone else.

"Hi." Callie glanced at her watch, her first patient was Mr Herring, inevitably, and she could see he was already waiting and watching closely lest someone be given preferential treatment and get in before him. "Follow me," she said to the crime scene photographer and couldn't suppress a little smile of satisfaction as she saw the look of outrage on Mr Herring's face.

"Thank you for seeing me, Dr Hughes," Lisa said as soon as they were in Callie's consulting room and the door was closed.

"Not at all, thank you for doing that photograph for me. It really helped."

"I thought no one recognised it."

"Well, no, but it helped in that it eliminated him as a local."

"Okay, good." Lisa didn't seem sure how to proceed.

"Although putting the picture on the news hasn't helped either."

"So, I heard."

There were a few moments of silence.

"Tell me what you want to say, Lisa, I have a waiting room full of patients out there." Not strictly true, but Callie felt she had to hurry things up.

"I'm not a racist," Lisa blurted out, and Callie resisted the urge to reply that all racists say that. "I was at the rally, just to find out what was going on," she continued.

"It's none of my business why you were there, Lisa. I don't have to remind you that I was there too."

"Yes, but everyone knows you've got an Asian boyfriend, so no one's going to think you were there that night because you're a member of the FNM."

Callie wasn't surprised it was common knowledge that she was going out with Billy Iqbal.

"Whereas anyone who knows you were there, would?"

Lisa nodded and then shook her head, as well.

"Close friends would know I'm not racist, but others, at work, might think I was. I don't advertise my views and some of them are… you know, they might think I agreed with them."

The suggestion seemed to be that there were some FNM sympathisers in the lab, which concerned Callie. If there was a culture of racism, it could affect their work, not to mention any colleagues that were people of colour.

Callie would have liked to ask for more details but Lisa looked miserable and Callie took pity on her. For now.

"So why were you there? What were you hoping to find out?"

"If they had any connections to Claybourne." Lisa almost spat out the name.

"The FNM? What makes you think he has anything to do with them? Apart from the fact he was at the rally."

"Because Claybourne's an evil bastard."

"Much as I might agree that he's no saint, why do you think he's evil? I mean, that's a very strong word."

"It's the only word for him." Lisa closed her eyes and shook her head, before deciding to tell Callie. "He and my dad were in business together, back when I was a kid. Claybourne tricked my dad out of his half of the arcade. He told everyone he bought my dad out, but he didn't. My dad got nothing. It ruined him, cost him his marriage and he never recovered. He died last year, cirrhosis of the liver."

"So now you are looking to get your own back and find something to ruin Claybourne with?"

Lisa nodded and Callie saw a tear run down her cheek.

"Look, Lisa," Callie said. "Going to an FNM rally isn't going to ruin him, he could claim, like you, that he was only there on a fact-finding mission."

"But his thugs beat up that other man."

"Who has chosen not to press charges."

"I know he's into all that though, I just know it!"

The woman was clearly desperate to find something she could use against the councillor.

Callie's desk phone rang as the receptionist reminded her that she should have started surgery and that Mr Herring was waiting.

"Just tell him I'm dealing with an emergency," Callie told her and turned back to Lisa who was standing, ready to leave.

"I'm sorry, you're busy–" she said going to the door.

"No, wait." Callie stopped her. "If I tell you that Claybourne is being investigated by the police for another matter…"

Callie crossed her fingers as Lisa looked at her, a gleam of hope in her eyes. She hoped the photographer wouldn't ask her what, as she knew full well that there was nothing concrete to link him to the cigarette smuggling without Morris, so any investigation would likely be dropped.

"...and that I will do my best to make sure that they pursue it, would you do something for me?" Callie continued.

"Is this about the cigarette smuggling?"

"How do you know about that?" Callie reacted sharply.

Lisa thought for a moment before telling her.

"My boyfriend works for the council, they've been trying to link Claybourne to it, but haven't got anywhere."

"Did you know about the raid?"

"God no, he wouldn't tell me anything about it. He knows how I feel. I wouldn't have been able to keep away."

"Good. We'll need to tread carefully. Will you help me?"

"If you can pin anything on that slippery bugger, I'll do anything I can."

"Yes, well, this is to do with body number nine rather than Claybourne."

Lisa looked disappointed.

"Okay." She shrugged. "I'll still help you."

"Brilliant!" Callie beamed. "Do you know about aging photographs?"

"I did a course, a while back, but I'm no expert." Lisa's interest had been piqued.

"But you could have a go?"

"Yes, I could do. But why do you want me to make the man in the photo look older?"

"Younger. I'd like you to make him look younger. Maybe early teens?"

"That's harder."

"But you could try?"

Lisa thought for a moment before nodding.

"That's great. Then we can see if anyone recognises him as a younger boy."

"Provided you can get the police to release it." Lisa still seemed dubious about Callie's plan.

"Don't worry, that's down to me to try and persuade them." Callie sounded more confident than she actually was, but she had plans to work on Miller. "And I won't forget about Claybourne, either."

Chapter 22

Despite considerable research on the internet, reports of how Claybourne had come to own the amusement arcade, or rather how his wife had come to own it, were few and far between.

"There has to be something in what Lisa was telling me," Callie said to Billy as they shared a bottle of wine and a home-made Thai green curry later that night. The curry was delicious and Callie realised, with a slight feeling of guilt, that Billy was a much better cook than she would ever be.

"It's a sad story, but it's hard to know for sure what really happened."

"I know. But Lisa clearly thinks Claybourne is responsible for her dad's death, morally if not physically."

"It might be worth checking if there was an inquest, as there might be some comment on the circumstances of his death."

"No inquest. I checked. He'd been ill a long time by the time he died."

"Then you are going to have to either have a dig around in the property archives, which may tell you little more than that ownership passed from one person to the next, or get some local gossip."

It was frustrating, Callie thought as she cleared away the remains of their meal and loaded the dishwasher. And her hopes for getting a picture of body number nine as a boy were not looking good. Billy had already warned her, as Lisa had, that making people look younger in photographs, particularly trying to guess how they looked as children, was much less successful than aging them.

It seemed as if all her possible leads were turning into dead-ends, but Callie refused to be down-hearted. Kate would probably be able to help her with her search through the archives, and she might be able to find something about it in the local papers from the time. Heartened by at least a vague plan she could follow up the next day, Callie went back to Billy; after all, she didn't know how much longer she might have with him, so she had better make the most of that time.

* * *

Her regular weekend brunch in The Land of Green Ginger with Kate was as good as ever and the two friends parted with Kate promising to look up any information about the amusement arcade and any changes of ownership, with the warning that it would simply be ownership information and none of the story behind any changes. Callie knew she was right and so she made her way to the library to trawl through old copies of the local paper. While they would still be constrained by libel laws, they might hint at the relationship between Claybourne and Furnow and what had caused their falling out. Having spent nearly two hours working through them on a computer she gave up. Whilst there was no shortage of pictures of the councillor — opening a new crazy golf park, shaking hands with the mayor, or handing out prizes at a school — there was little in the papers about the change in ownership of the arcade or any of Claybourne's business ventures.

"You could try the local history group," the helpful librarian suggested when Callie told her that she was looking for information about the history of the amusement arcade by the pier and how little she had found. "I know they tend to be interested in things from further back in time, but there might be someone who knows about it."

It seemed like a good idea, so Callie made her way back to the Old Town and Hastings History House, a small museum in Courthouse Street where the local history group was based.

Going through the small glass door, Callie was ashamed to realise that despite living in the town all these years, she had never been inside the house. She was fascinated by the displays and information about the town through the ages that she found, and soon got talking to an elderly man who was there to answer questions from the public, and make sure than no one made off with any of the exhibits.

"I was actually looking for information about the history of the amusement arcade, and its ownership over the years," she explained to the man who had introduced himself as Mr Simpson.

"Which one?" he asked.

"The one opposite the funfair," she explained.

"That's relatively new," he continued, dismissively. "Only built in the sixties. Now the one in George Street has more history—"

"So, who developed the seafront along there?" Callie managed to stop him, gently, and steer him back to talking about the arcade owned by Claybourne.

"I see." He smiled. "You are you are interested in the post-war developments of Hastings then." Mr Simpson then went off into a long discourse about poor planning decisions and the clearing of slums to make way for the new London Road. Callie realised that he would soon get onto the sheer vandalism of building a shopping centre on the cricket pitch if she didn't stop him quickly.

"I'm really only interested in the arcade development, perhaps you could put me onto someone who might know about it, if you don't?"

He looked affronted.

"It's not really historic. Why on earth would you be interested in that?"

"Family history," she replied, not mentioning that it wasn't her family she was talking about.

"Well, I don't know that anyone—"

"Dr Hughes!"

Callie and Mr Simpson both turned and Callie smiled to see a patient of hers, Harry Wardle coming towards them.

"Do let me show you our new exhibit, Doctor." Wardle firmly took her elbow and led her away from Mr Simpson. "Boring old fart," he whispered by way of explanation as they walked to the back of the room and he pointed to an early photograph of a fisherman mending his nets, pretending to be telling her about it.

"So, I gathered," Callie whispered back in a conspiratorial way.

"Now what can I help you with?" he asked.

Callie again explained her interest in the arcade.

"I'm afraid Mr Simpson is right, it's not really history," Wardle told her with a smile. "Not when I remember it so well. Now, are you wanting the official facts or the gossip? Because if it's the latter, I suggest we go to the café on the corner and discuss it over a pot of tea."

Which is exactly what they did.

"You should have told our Mr Simpson that you are a GP and he could have given you all the gory details about his hernia op," Wardle teased her.

"That's exactly why I tend not to let on about it. I get quite enough of that at work." Callie laughed.

"So, why are you interested in the gossip about the arcade?" he asked her in a more serious tone as they sipped their tea and Wardle ate a toasted tea cake that was dripping with butter.

Callie hesitated.

"I can't really tell you that. I'm sorry."

"Ah, I suppose it has something to do with your other job, the police work. Not to worry." He took another sip of tea. "Now, let me see. Eric Furnow was a jobbing builder, and not very good at it, either. Never had two pennies to rub together, and when he did, he spent it all on drink. Then, one miraculous day, he won the pools. Suddenly, he seemed to have a lot of friends he'd never had before. Peter Claybourne was one of them."

"Let me guess, Claybourne persuaded Furnow to buy the arcade."

Wardle nodded.

"Well, the building, anyway, it wasn't an arcade then. And Peter helped Eric get all the permissions he needed for change of use. To be fair, Eric would never have been able to manage that himself."

"So Claybourne did legitimately help?"

"Absolutely, can't take that away from the man." Wardle looked as if he would have liked to do just that. "As I said, Eric was a drinker and suddenly he had loads of money to do it. He spent most of his time in the pubs, buying everyone drinks, and giving money away. Most sensible thing Maggie did was divorce him. She had a small child to think of and the settlement meant that she was at least able to buy her own home, and put a bit of money away, out of Eric's reach, because he worked his way through the rest pretty quick."

"But he still had the arcade?"

"Yes, that was up and running by then, and managed by Peter Claybourne, but apparently, wasn't making any money." Wardle gave her a long look. "Seemed busy enough to me."

"You think Claybourne was cheating Eric Furnow?"

"That's a strong word." He hesitated before continuing. "But, let's face it, it wouldn't have been hard."

"What happened after that?"

"Eric was seriously unwell by then. There's only so long you can drink like that before your body gives up on you. He was running up tabs in pubs all over town and was about to lose his home as well, but Claybourne came up with a plan to pay off his debts."

"In exchange for the arcade?"

Wardle nodded and topped up their cups from the teapot.

"Well, it wasn't making any money according to the books, so it seemed like a good idea to Eric. To be honest, anything that kept the alcohol flowing looked good to Eric by that time."

"And then, surprise, surprise, the arcade starts making money."

"Exactly. Even Eric could see that he'd been conned, but there was nothing he could do, it was all legal."

"It must have devastated him."

"Drank himself to death within a few months. All very sad. You know, we can all criticise Claybourne for what he did, but the outcome was always going to be the same for Eric Furnow once he won that money."

They sat in silence for a few moments, drinking their tea and thinking about a life so comprehensively destroyed by coming into money and meeting an unscrupulous man.

Chapter 23

When Callie looked at the photograph that Lisa had emailed to her, she was amazed. She was looking at the picture of a young boy, eleven or twelve years old, but she could still recognise him as the man he had grown into. She didn't know how Lisa had done it, but the end result was stunning. Callie just hoped that it was recognisable and that she could persuade Miller to give it to the press. Perhaps a family would finally know what happened to their little boy.

"Hi, Nigel?" she said when the incident room phone was finally answered. "I've just sent you a reworked photo of body number nine as a young boy that the forensic lab has been working on." She hoped no one checked whether or not it was officially their work, rather than a side-project of Lisa's. "I was wondering if you could show it to DI Miller and see if he would be willing to run it in the press?"

"Erm, he's a bit busy at the moment, Dr Hughes."

"Well, can someone else do it?"

"Not really."

Callie could almost hear Nigel squirming and blushing at the other end of the phone.

"Don't worry, I'll come in and speak to him myself."

"No! Not just now," DC Nugent blurted out in a panic and Callie suddenly realised she could hear shouting in the background. It was hard to work out exactly what was being said by the woman doing the shouting, but she did not sound calm. The voice got louder as the woman presumably got closer to Nigel's desk.

"So, you can just go back to your whore—"

"Lizzie, look—"

"And don't think I'm coming back!"

There was the sound of the door slamming and a few moments' silence. Callie had been hoping that Steve Miller would have managed to convince his wife Lizzie that the compromising photos of him had been sent to her by someone trying to discredit him by now, but it seemed that he hadn't been successful if the very public argument she had heard was anything to go by.

"So, um, I don't think now is a good time," DC Nugent said quickly, and Callie had to agree. There was no way Miller would be in the mood to discuss anything with her after that. He would be way too embarrassed and angry. Callie would need to wait until he had calmed down, at least a little.

"Oh, Dr Hughes?" DC Nugent said in little more than a whisper. "I have a message for you. Just a moment while I find it."

She waited as he sorted through what she knew was likely to be hundreds of message slips on his desk.

"Ah, yes, here it is. Mr Savage's assistant called and asked you to give her a ring. I have the number here."

Callie made a note of the number as she wondered why on earth Mrs Savage might want her to call. There was only one way to find out.

"Hello? Mrs Savage? It's Dr Hughes here, I had a message to call you."

"Oh, yes, Dr Hughes." If Mrs Savage was pleased to hear from Callie, she hid it well. "My husband thought you might be interested in a meeting he's holding tonight, to discuss the important topic of immigration and those trying to cross illegally from France. It's at the Broomgrove Community Centre in Ore, seven-thirty."

"Oh, that's very kind of him, and you, to think of me." Callie thought about it for a moment. "Yes, I would be interested."

"Good, I'll see you there tonight, Dr Hughes, goodbye." She ended the call.

Callie was surprised, she had thought that the MP, and his wife, would happily never see her again. Perhaps he was determined to win her over, unlikely as that was, but the opportunity to hear more of his views on the dead migrants was one she did not want to miss.

* * *

The community centre was modern and purpose-built and clean. There were quite a few cars in the carpark, including the little red one she had seen at Ted Savage's office, so Callie was hopeful that the meeting would be well-attended.

She went to the reception desk and saw that there were a number of events taking place, there were posters for slimming clubs, Pilates and even a reading group. Callie asked where she would find her meeting and was directed to a small room, with a couple of dozen plastic chairs set out in preparation. There was a table at the front, with three more chairs, and a jug of water and two glasses. Clearly one of the speakers was not expected to want a drink.

Callie glanced at her watch. It was five minutes before the meeting was due to start but only half a dozen or so people were already there waiting. Perhaps Savage's eagerness to get her to the meeting was more about not wanting to speak to an empty room than because he thought she might really be interested.

Callie took a seat in the back row of chairs and looked around at the others waiting for the meeting to begin. A middle-aged lady seated at the front was wearing a dog collar and a benign expression. There were a group of three students, an elderly couple and a man who seemed to be asleep. It didn't look as though it was going to be a very lively meeting, but just as she wondered if it would be cancelled or if perhaps she should sneak out and give it a miss, the door opened and four men came into the room. One of them was Councillor Claybourne and the others looked very much like the men who had been with him at the FNM rally and who had laid into David Morris.

Everyone turned and looked at the new arrivals, apart from the man who was asleep, and there was a general air of unease as the group took their seats in the middle of the room. There was no way Callie was going to leave now, although she did check how close she was to the way out, just in case it turned out to be a more exciting evening than she had expected!

At seven-thirty, exactly, a door at the back of the room opened and Ted Savage, his wife and a thin man who Callie did not recognise, came in and took their places behind the table. It was the thin man who started the meeting, standing up and introducing both himself, as the local constituency chairperson, and Ted Savage as the MP. Mrs Savage was seated to one side of the table and clearly wasn't worthy of an introduction. She looked around the room, checking out every person and smiling at them, although the smile looked a bit strained when she saw Claybourne, and Callie. Then she dutifully took out a notepad and pen, making it clear she was at the meeting in her role as an assistant rather than a wife.

Once introduced by his chairperson, Savage stood to talk to the people in the room. Smiling genuinely and engaging with everyone, apart from Claybourne and his group, who he studiously ignored. It was interesting that they clearly knew each other. Claybourne, for his part, sat with his arms crossed and a smirk on his face.

Savage was a good speaker, talking eloquently about the suffering around the world, telling them that people needed to find a safe place to live, that they had a right to it and that we, as a rich country, had a duty to help. He touched on the tragedy of those who had drowned trying to reach the safety of our shores and explained that he had spoken with the prime minister about how having a more open immigration policy and allowing a greater number of refugees to claim asylum could help reduce people trafficking and so stop the dangerous flow of migrants coming across the Channel.

He got an enthusiastic round of applause from his wife, the students and the vicar, but it wasn't loud enough to wake the sleeping man.

At the end of his talk, Savage turned to leave, but Claybourne sprang to his feet.

"Not going to open the floor to questions?" Claybourne asked. "I didn't have you down as a coward, Ted."

Savage turned back, with a resigned look on his face.

"I am happy to answer reasonable questions, Councillor, but I won't stand for any abuse."

"Abuse? I'm not here to abuse anyone. I'm just here to put the working man's point of view."

"What makes you their representative?" It wasn't Savage who asked the question but one of the students.

"At least I am one of them, not just a parasite living off my parents while pretending to study art."

Callie wondered if Claybourne actually knew the girl as her face flushed, suggesting his barb had hit home. Claybourne turned back to Savage.

"The working man, from Hastings that is, has a right to a job, and a home too, you know. Bleeding-heart liberals like yourself, who want to take in all-comers, people who've never lived in this country, never paid taxes here and who will overwhelm our NHS, you will deprive the rest of us of our rights. Rights that we've worked and paid for."

There was a murmur of agreement from Claybourne's cronies.

"Of course, Hastings' people have the right to a job and a home here, and we need to make sure that they have them," Savage answered, surprisingly evenly. "And we have to make sure that the NHS can cope, as well, but some of these people have been through hell, their homes and families have been destroyed. They are in fear for their lives. They have rights too, they have the right to life – everyone has the right to that."

Whilst Savage was being remarkably controlled, his chairperson was clearly worried by the confrontation and trying to usher him out. Interestingly, it was Mrs Savage who seemed most angry at the disruption, glaring first at Claybourne and then at her husband, as if he should take control and stop the discussion.

"And what if your constituents disagree? Are you prepared to stake your career on that?" Claybourne asked Savage.

"Yes," Savage replied and he turned to leave the room.

"We'll see what they say come election day, then," Claybourne called after him as Savage left the room, his wife and the constituency chairperson scuttling after him, Mrs Savage looking more than a little rattled by the exchange.

Claybourne clearly felt he had had the better of the argument and left the meeting room grinning like a Cheshire cat, his entourage following closely behind. As everyone else, apart from the slumbering man, left the room, Callie sat for a moment or two, trying to work out what had been going on. It was clear that Claybourne was very much opposed to Savage's stance on the migrants and it looked to her like he might even be preparing to stand against the sitting MP at the next election.

She was about to leave herself when the door at the back of the room opened again and the constituency chairperson stuck his head out. Seeing her and also that the room was effectively empty, he scurried over.

"Um, Dr Hughes, glad I caught you. I wonder if you have a moment?"

She stood and followed him through the door to a small, spartan office where Mr and Mrs Savage sat. Whilst his wife was nursing a cup of tea, Callie could see that the MP had an amber liquid in his mug and a hip flask was on the table in front of him.

"Ah, thank you for coming, Dr Hughes." Savage stood and indicated a chair for her to sit.

"I'll get off now, Ted. Don't you worry about Claybourne, he's nothing but a windbag, he'll lose his deposit if he stands against you."

The thin man waved a vague goodbye and left the room, confirming Callie's thoughts that Claybourne was planning a move to be the next MP. She sincerely hoped that Miller, or Trading Standards were able to link him to the cigarette smuggling and effectively end his political ambitions by putting him in jail. She didn't like him one bit. Savage took a sip of his whisky and smiled at Callie.

"You must be wondering why I asked you to come this evening."

"I have to admit, I was surprised."

"It's because you were right." He looked at her intently. "And I wanted to come clean. Tell all."

He almost seemed to be flirting with Callie which was strange as his wife was sitting next to her. Callie stole a quick look at the woman and could see that she wasn't happy. Whether it was because her husband was flirting or because he was about to say something she didn't approve of, Callie wasn't sure.

Callie turned back to the MP and smiled encouragingly. She felt sufficiently sure that he wouldn't pounce with his wife in the room, although, given some of the stories she had heard about politicians, perhaps that was naive of her.

"I did indeed give the reporter the question that I wanted him to ask."

Callie and Mrs Savage both seemed to sigh with slight relief. Indeed, Mrs Savage seemed suddenly quite relaxed, compared to her normal rather uptight demeanour, and she even took a sip of tea.

"And why did you do that?" Callie asked him.

"Because I wanted to answer it."

Callie felt that was a very inadequate reply.

"But you knew that the boat had not been sabotaged."

"No, no, I had no information on its condition."

Which was a typical politician's answer, Callie thought, neither confirming nor denying.

"You had no reason to suspect that it had been damaged."

"Well, you might say that, but it capsized, or sank, or whatever, so it might well have been sabotaged," he said.

"Or it might just have been unseaworthy, or unsuitable for the conditions, and overloaded with people who had no idea about boats, navigation, tides or just how treacherous the sea can be."

"It seems to me, that it amounts to much the same thing. Young men died and someone else was to blame."

"Yes, but by suggesting the boat had been deliberately damaged, you implied that in some way, a far-right group, possibly even the FNM could have been responsible. You made out they were murderers," Callie said.

"It is, I suppose, possible that people could have misinterpreted the situation, yes, and I must take the blame for that and the subsequent disruption of the FNM rally, I suppose. But I can't say that I'm sorry. The whole reason they were having the rally was to celebrate the death of those men, and to capitalise on the situation. You can't believe that was right."

Callie held up her hands in mock surrender.

"Of course not! But your actions could have caused a riot. Could have got more people hurt or even killed."

He waved away her concerns, dismissively.

"Dixon and Claybourne are just thugs. They might be a bit heavy-handed, but they wouldn't want anything serious to happen. They'd never get elected if it did."

Callie realised that he was disappointed about that. When he hinted at the FNM involvement in the deaths of the migrants in the interview, he had hoped there might be serious unrest at the rally and that maybe his actions would not just disrupt the proceedings, but also damage the political ambitions of the organisers.

"So why are you telling me all this?"

"I wanted you to understand what I was trying to do, and what the consequences of men like Claybourne and Dixon getting into power would be."

"I know that already."

"And that it's important they are stopped." He leant forward, eyes boring into her. "It's important that the police do not take sides. You do realise that more anti-fascists were arrested at the rally than members of Dixon's mob?"

"No," she replied coolly, beginning to understand what he wanted from her.

"Of course, the police have a history of being—" He stopped, sensing she wasn't happy with the way the conversation was going. "It would be good to know there was someone there who was putting the alternate view, who could remind them that they need to be impartial."

There was no doubting his sincerity.

"Whilst I can assure you of my own impartiality," she responded, "telling the police how they need to behave really isn't my role." And she stood up to leave, hoping that he took the hint and didn't seriously expect her to be his mole or whatever it was he thought she might be and to her relief he just nodded and stood up as well.

"Good. I just wanted you to know that I believe in the sanctity of life. Of all lives, equally. As I am sure you do too." He grabbed her hand and shook it, then glanced at his wife, as if expecting her to show Callie out, but she was still sitting, gripping her teacup, white-knuckled.

"Teresa?" he said sharply.

She started at his voice, a small amount of tea spilling down the front of her pristine white shirt.

"Oh, oh dear!" she said and fussed about, putting down her tea and mopping at her shirt with a tissue, as her husband looked on with an expression of surprise. Callie made her way to the door.

"Goodbye, Dr Hughes," she finally managed to say to Callie's retreating back and hurried after her to show her out.

Callie wondered what sort of conversation would be going on in the room now she had left and the door had been firmly closed behind her.

Chapter 24

Callie suppressed a faint feeling of nausea as she followed the receptionist down the utilitarian school corridor. Schools still smelled the same as when she had been a student, even if she had been at a small private school rather than the large academy that she was currently visiting. A trip to see the headmistress or principal as they now seemed to like to be called, was still as frightening.

Resisting the urge to pull down her skirt or fidget, Callie waited in the comfortable chair outside the office as instructed. She was pleased not to be kept waiting long as patience had never been one of her strengths. The principal turned out to be a very smartly dressed woman in her forties. Callie could only admire women who managed to have demanding jobs but kept themselves immaculately groomed and somehow managed to do it all in high heels. Perhaps she had a pair of comfy slippers hidden under the desk.

"I'm so pleased you've come to see us," the principal said to her once they were settled in her office. It looked like every headteacher's office Callie had ever been in: a bookcase laden with suitably serious tomes and a variety of cups and awards displayed, framed certificates hung on the walls along with photographs of the principal with a number of local dignitaries, including both Councillor Claybourne and Ted Savage MP. "The um, coroner's officer said that you would be in touch."

"It's very good of you to respond so quickly."

"Well, it won't have escaped your notice that one of our students has died, Dr Hughes."

"And two others have been near misses."

"Exactly. So, we'll take all the help we can get. I absolutely don't want any more tragedies."

She seemed genuinely to be concerned for her pupils rather than the school's reputation, although the two obviously went hand in hand.

"Do you have any idea why this has happened?" Callie asked her.

"I rather thought that was more your area of expertise."

"I rather hoped you might be able to help." Callie smiled to remove any sting from her words, she needed this woman onside. "Anything that could help us get an answer to why these young girls are abusing their medication."

The principal hesitated before answering.

"One of the teachers caught a boy acting suspiciously and when she searched his bag, found, amongst other banned substances, several asthma inhalers. We do not have asthma listed as one of his many problems," she added, drily.

"He was selling them?"

"That would be the implication. He has been suspended pending review of his case, and past problems we have had with him, and I will be recommending permanent exclusion."

Callie sat back. An illicit trade in inhalers made little sense to her, but she would research it, find out why it might be and if it was a problem elsewhere.

"Okay, I'll speak to the asthma consultant who has agreed to come with me to give a talk and confirm the date with your secretary. We might need to change what we say slightly, in light of your information."

"Yes. That's very kind of you. I don't want you to get the impression that we have a big drug problem here, but—"

"Every school has some, I do understand that, but that's also why it's important for us to try and nip whatever is going on here in the bud."

"Exactly." The principal seemed happy with that.

* * *

Once back at the surgery, Callie asked her colleagues, but none of them had ever heard of asthma inhalers being sold by drug dealers, or could think of any reason why they might be. Even a search online wasn't very helpful, there was a suggestion that the use of inhalers before taking other drugs might enhance their effect simply by expanding the airways. Apparently, there was a "rush" rather than a "high" from overuse, probably because it made the heart beat faster, but everywhere agreed, there was little real effect, apart from the problem of reducing sensitivity to the drugs that might save an asthmatic who was having an attack.

At a loss to know what on earth was going on at the school, Callie left a message for the consultant to call her and discuss their upcoming visit. She also managed to get hold of Anna's mother, and asked her to talk to her daughter and see if she could find out why the girl was using so much and why her friends seemed to be doing the same.

That done, she settled down to an uneventful surgery. It wasn't until she was just finishing off the last few bits of paperwork that either person got back to her.

The consultant wasn't really able to enlighten her on reasons for the abuse of inhalers.

"I have heard that teenagers that abuse drugs are more likely to misuse their inhalers too," he told her. "So perhaps you are right, perhaps they believe it will give them a bigger hit or something. I'll talk to my colleagues, see if anyone has any ideas."

But Mrs Thompson's reply to her earlier call was much more illuminating.

"Right, Dr Hughes," she started. "The preventer inhaler, it's a steroid, isn't it?"

"Well, generally, yes," Callie replied cautiously.

"And steroids cause weight gain, right?"

"Well, no, not these sorts of steroids and anyway, the dose is tiny, just a few micrograms."

"Oh, well that seems to be Anna's concern."

"She thinks she'll put on weight if she uses her preventer inhaler?"

"That's right. You know how sensitive she is about her weight."

"All teenage girls are."

"Goes with the territory," Mrs Thompson agreed.

"So where do you think this information came from?"

"She just said 'everyone knows' and 'dunno' when I asked her that."

"Okay, well, at least I have something to go on now. Thank you. Please tell Anna that she needs to use her preventer and reassure her that they won't make her put on weight. I'll get onto the local asthma consultant and tell him what's going on. We're due to speak at a school assembly later this week, so we'll focus on that particular bit of misinformation. That's been really helpful. Thank you."

And it had. Although, as she explained to Billy later, it didn't entirely explain why the school drug dealer had so many salbutamol inhalers in his possession.

"He was probably just taking advantage of the situation. Supply and demand."

"But how would he get hold of a regular supply?"

"Recruit all the asthmatics he knows and get them to over-order."

Callie gave that some thought, it seemed pretty devious, but actually quite easy to do.

"Perhaps if I could speak with the lad who was dealing…" she mused.

"You'll be lucky to find out who it is. Can't see the school releasing his name to you."

Callie knew Billy was right, she had to find another way of identifying him, and stopping him from continuing to sell inhalers. His actions might have contributed to the death of one girl already and nearly killed another. She made a mental note to speak to the consultant again before their talk at the school. They needed to make sure they made it clear that steroid inhalers did not cause weight gain.

Chapter 25

Just as she was due to leave for work the next morning, Callie got a text from Miller suggesting they meet for lunch. There was also a message from DC Nugent telling her to watch breakfast television.

Switching on the TV as she said goodbye to Billy, Callie saw the picture of the young boy on the screen.

"Is that the age regression pic your mate at the lab did for body number nine?" Billy asked, pausing at the door.

"Yes. It is." Callie turned the sound up.

"Police in Hastings are asking for help in identifying a body that was found on the beach at about the same time as the terrible tragedy of the migrant boat capsize. They believe one of the young men found was not from that boat and earlier, I spoke to Detective Inspector Miller about the reasons why."

The picture changed to a pre-recorded section where Miller stood, looking slightly uncomfortable, in front of Hastings' main police station.

"We believe that one of the bodies found on the beach at Fairlight might not be that of a migrant and that he may be connected to the body of a young woman, identified as Michelle Carlisle, found later. No one has come forward to identify this young man and we have come to believe that it is possible he has been missing for some considerable time, perhaps living rough, or in a squat, in London. Given that his family may not have seen him since he was a teenager, or younger, we have done an age regression picture of him in the hope that someone may recognise him from this."

The sanitised picture of body nine, as he was now, and the picture of him as he might have looked as a young boy were then flashed up on screen. The presenter then finished with another plea for anyone recognising either picture to get in touch and giving out the phone numbers for them to do so.

"Well that should get them a few phone calls," Billy said before giving her another quick kiss on the cheek and hurrying out to work.

Callie thought that that was probably an understatement.

* * *

The café where she had agreed to meet Miller was near the pier, and Callie walked past the amusement arcade on her way. She was surprised to see Peter Claybourne standing outside the arcade, almost as if he was waiting for her. He waved and smiled as she passed. No, Callie thought, that wasn't a smile it was more of a smirk, just like the one he had had on his face at the MP's meeting, and made her feel that he knew something that she didn't. And that she wasn't going to like it when she found out.

If so, he would have been right.

"The Superintendent has had a complaint," he said between hurried mouthfuls of a cheese omelette washed down with black coffee. Sergeant Jeffries was eating a full English, including fried bread and black pudding and had an extra-large mug of tea to go with it. The speed at which he was shovelling it into his mouth made Callie alarmed for his digestion if not his cardiovascular system, but at the moment the only casualty seemed to be his tie, which had a blob of egg yolk sliming its way slowly down it.

"Oh yes? Who from?" Callie asked, although she had a pretty good idea.

"Councillor Claybourne."

"Man's a tosser," Jeffries added.

"What am I supposed to have done now?"

"Harassed him," Jeffries grinned as he told her.

"Not sexually," Miller clarified quickly.

Callie suppressed a shudder at the thought.

"Did you follow him to a meeting he was attending the night before last?" Miller asked her.

"No!" she replied. "I was invited to attend by Ted Savage. I had no idea Claybourne was going to be there."

"And you didn't go into his arcade and question the staff?"

"I asked the girl in the change kiosk how I could get to see him," she replied, irritated. "And, before you ask, I may have taken the opportunity to put a couple of other questions to her while I was there."

"And you told Trading Standards he was involved in the cigarette smuggling."

"No. I told them he might have been involved but I didn't have any proof, it's not the same thing at all."

Miller sighed.

The waitress came over with a cup of tea and a plate of salad at that moment and they all waited until the woman had gone. Jeffries eyed Callie's lunch with distaste before wiping the last of his fried bread round his plate to pick up the last of the egg and bacon grease.

"Perhaps you could try and keep your distance from the man for a while?" Miller suggested.

"It's not my fault we ended up at the same meeting. I could accuse him of following me. After all, I arrived before he did."

"Yes, but he hasn't suggested you have committed a crime."

"Yes, he has." Callie was really indignant now. "He's suggested I'm harassing him."

Miller sighed again and rubbed his chest.

"Heartburn?" she suggested.

"Are you surprised?"

She wasn't, what with all the work pressures and the state of his marriage, but it seemed unfair that Jeffries, gulping the last of his tea, appeared completely unaffected by his enormous and unhealthy lunch.

"Anyway," Miller said, pushing back his chair and making to leave. "Don't go anywhere near him, not unless you want to wind up being arrested."

"Wait!" Callie stopped him. "How is the investigation going?"

He looked surprised.

"I've just told you to keep away from Claybourne. And anyway, there's no evidence whatsoever to link him to the smuggling."

"No, not that investigation. The one into the migrants. And the unidentified man."

"Oh," he said and sat down again. Jeffries had the advantage of not having started to stand as yet.

"We think we've identified the boat the migrants came over on before transferring to the RIB, but that's been taken over by border police and the French. The Red Cross is taking the lead in identifying the migrants who died."

"So that just leaves you with identifying body number nine and finding his and Michelle Carlisle's killer."

"Yes."

"Had a lot of calls about the photo," Jeffries said helpfully.

"But it's too early to know if any of them are useful," Miller added firmly and stood again. This time he meant to leave.

Callie took her paper napkin and leant towards Jeffries.

"Here," she said as she wiped the worst of the egg yolk off his tie.

"Oh." He looked surprised as if he had no idea how the stain had got there. "Cheers, Doc."

Chapter 26

There was no doubt in Callie's mind that Claybourne was the man behind the cigarette smuggling. She believed David Morris on that front, and that the councillor's complaint to the Superintendent was nothing more than a ploy to discourage her from investigating his connection to it any further.

Little did he know that it was the one thing most likely to increase the chances of her doing just that. She hated bullying and that was exactly what she felt he was trying to do. She did concede, even to herself, however, that he wasn't part of the people smuggling as the boat definitely seemed to have ended up in Hastings by mistake, but, as it also seemed that body number nine was also not part of the people smuggling, there was always the chance that he was connected to the cigarettes and so to Claybourne, one way or another.

"Honestly, the man's a sleazeball," Callie said after explaining her theory to Kate over a drink in The Stag later that night.

"I'm not arguing with you," Kate replied. "But you have to remember that the man has power and he has it in for you already."

"He's a local councillor, that's not real power."

"Like, ooh, let me see, who has real power? Oh yes, an MP." Kate grinned. "Is he as sexy in real life as he is on TV?"

Callie thought about that for a moment.

"You know, I hadn't really given it much thought. Yes, he has bags of charm, but is he sexy? Not in my book."

"Why ever not?"

Callie shrugged.

"Maybe he's not my type."

"Or maybe you are too much in lurve with Dr Iqbal to notice other men." Kate sighed. "I have never been in that position."

"In love with Dr Iqbal?"

"No." Kate giggled. "So in love that I didn't notice other men, silly."

Callie knew that her friend didn't have a good track record on fidelity, so she chose to say nothing. It was something that she couldn't understand. She had always been serially monogamous, whereas Kate often seemed to be running two or three boyfriends simultaneously.

"Getting back to Councillor Claybourne…"

"Do we have to?"

"Yes. I mean, seriously, he made a complaint to the Superintendent – my boss, as far as me being a police doctor is concerned. He could have damaged my career, may already have done so."

Kate looked at her thoughtfully.

"You are right."

"And he intimated that he would be running against Ted Savage at the next election."

"You can't honestly believe he'd win?"

"I'm not prepared to take the chance."

"Oh dear, where is this leading, Callie?"

"If he's charged with the cigarette racket, he'll lose his seat on the council and won't be able to stand as a candidate."

"Isn't that bullying, Callie?"

Even though Kate had a twinkle in her eye that told Callie she wasn't serious, Callie gave it some thought.

"No, it isn't. He's the one who is breaking the law and thinking he can ride roughshod over everyone else. I'd just be exposing the truth."

"And tell me, dear friend of mine, just how exactly are you going to do that?"

Callie had to concede that it was a good question. A very good question indeed.

* * *

It was a question that Callie spent a lot of time thinking about during the rest of the evening. Her one link, David Morris, had disappeared off, goodness knows where, and Callie could hardly blame him after the beating he had received.

The shop where she had seen Morris buy cigarettes was open but they were hardly likely to be selling the cigarettes again with the Trading Standards people already breathing down their necks. She couldn't understand how they had failed to find any stock when it was raided.

Unless they had been tipped off. But by whom? And how did they know the raid was going to take place?

Callie knew that Trading Standards was part of the council, was it too great a leap of the imagination to think that someone in that department tipped off Councillor Claybourne? The more Callie thought about it, the more she believed it was possible, and even likely. The trouble was, she couldn't just go to the head of Trading Standards and say she thought one of his team was corrupt. For all she knew, he, or she, could be the one.

She was going to have to find another way of implicating Claybourne in his illegal activities, and maybe, Callie conceded, that was a job for the police.

* * *

"I might not be investigating the people smuggling anymore, but I do still have two murders on the books," Miller complained.

Callie patted his hand soothingly.

"I know, and they obviously take precedence over a little matter of council corruption."

"Of which you have no proof whatsoever."

"Which is exactly why I need your help, or the help of one or two of your team."

"I can't just go loaning out my team to an investigation that isn't even official. Do you have any idea how much paperwork I have to fill in before I so much as ask one of them to leave the room?"

"Okay, when I said I needed the help of one or two of your team, I wasn't meaning me personally. I meant that the investigation into the smuggled cigarettes needed them."

"But that's not my case. It's Trading Standards'."

"And they aren't going to solve it if someone is helping Claybourne."

They seemed to be going round in circles.

"The best I can do is tell the Super we're looking into a possible leak in Trading Standards and maybe put together a sting operation."

Callie grinned.

"But only if it is simple."

She leant back, still smiling.

"And I can't guarantee he will go for it; in fact, I can almost guarantee he won't."

"But he might."

"Only if I don't mention Claybourne and keep your name out of it. So, do me a favour, Callie, don't go anywhere near him or any of his cronies. You hear me?"

Callie nodded.

"I promise. Scout's honour and all that."

He left and Callie uncrossed her fingers. She never had been a scout.

Chapter 27

Callie was surprised to see Anna Thompson in the waiting room when she went back to do her evening surgery. She looked tearful and Callie went straight over to her.

"Anna, what's the matter?"

Anna could only manage a sob in reply.

"Come into my room and tell me what's happened." She gave an apologetic shrug to the receptionist, who would have to field complaints about her running late, and led the teenager into her consulting room.

Callie busied herself getting a glass of water and some tissues for the girl, giving her time to get herself under control. When Anna had blown her nose and taken a gulp of water, Callie sat down and spoke to her.

"What's happened?" she asked.

"My friend, my best friend, Louise, she's in hospital, and I'm worried about her."

Callie could see where this conversation was going.

"And does she have asthma?"

Anna nodded.

"But she hasn't been using her preventer inhaler, like you?"

Anna nodded.

"Callum said we'd put on weight if we used them, but Mum says that's not true."

"It isn't. The dose of steroid you get in one of those inhalers is tiny because it goes straight to where it's needed."

"Oh." Anna seemed to understand.

"So, this Callum, what made him say that?"

Anna shifted uncomfortably in her seat.

"Dunno." She resorted to a teenager's favourite response when they believed to answer truthfully would get them in trouble.

"I think you do know, Anna. And I think you need to tell me. Think about your friend Louise and the other two girls who have already ended up in hospital. One of them died." Callie didn't like frightening the girl, but she really needed to get to the bottom of this before there was another death.

"He said we was helping them," Anna blurted out. "He said it was just because doctors wanted to save money that they wouldn't let us use the blue inhalers all the time."

"The blue inhalers are cheap as chips, Anna. It's the others that are more expensive. The reason we don't just give out the blue ones is because of exactly what has happened to your friend and what I have been warning could happen to you. You could have an acute asthma attack and the hospital won't be able to treat you because you are resistant to the drugs that could work. You have to listen to me."

"I'll be all right."

"Like Louise."

"She's different."

Callie had a sudden light-bulb moment.

"In that she really does have asthma."

Anna nodded.

"So how did you know how to fake asthma to get hold of the inhalers?"

"Callum's sister is a nurse. She told him that half the people doctors give inhalers to don't have asthma, it's just to keep them quiet."

"Did she also tell him that doctors won't keep on handing them out?"

"I dunno. Probably."

"And Callum thought up this way of making money? Tell girls the other inhalers would make them put on weight and then sell them the ones he got from you?"

Anna nodded.

"Only it wasn't just me. I found out he had a few of us getting them for him." She looked at Callie and a tear ran slowly down her face. "He told me I was special for getting them for him, but he had Beccy and Dawn doing it for him too, maybe others." She sobbed.

Callie patted her on the shoulder and handed the distraught girl another tissue. One dead, three more ending up in hospital, and what for? Money in the case of Callum, and feeling special in Anna's case. The question was, what was Callie to do about it? Besides speaking to the school and killing the myth of weight gain.

Maybe she needed to talk to a policeman. Or a lawyer.

* * *

"The trouble is always going to be proving that he did it knowingly," Kate explained to Callie over dinner at Porters. "I mean, obviously he can be done for illegally selling prescription drugs but I'd doubt the CPS would go for any charges like deliberate wounding or grievous bodily harm." She paused to cut herself a hefty mouthful of rare steak. "He could claim that he had no idea there would be consequences like that." She popped the steak in her mouth.

"Even if he got the idea about doing this from his sister who is a nurse?" Callie asked and realised she would have to wait a moment or two before Kate could answer, so she took the opportunity to tackle her cod fishcake.

"You would have to prove that she told him it could cause this situation, and I doubt she did, or would admit to it."

"So, what do you think I should do?"

"Exactly what you are doing. Speaking to the pupils. And it sounds as if at least one of his suppliers won't be helping him anymore."

"I've taken her off the asthma register and told the nurse about the scam; in case she has any other girls on the list who she thinks might be pulling the same trick."

"There you go then. You could also mention him to the community police, or even the drug squad. They may know who he is and be able to pay him a visit."

"Warn him off?"

"Exactly. Scare the pants off him. He's probably already thinking of his next money-making project. He sounds just the sort of shit to progress to major drug dealing if someone doesn't stop him now."

Callie wondered if her friend had already represented Callum in her professional role, or if it was just that she knew the sort of manipulative petty criminal he seemed to be.

"Right, it's a plan. More wine?" And Callie concentrated on enjoying herself for the rest of the evening.

Chapter 28

Getting into work nice and early the next day, Callie had time to make a couple of phone calls. As Kate had predicted, it turned out that both the community policeman and the drug squad were well acquainted with a lad called Callum, recently suspended from the school. They explained that whether or not they were able to arrest him for selling prescription drugs depended on them finding some on him, unless the headmistress was willing to act as a witness.

Reassured that, at the very least, he would get a warning, Callie felt she could safely leave the matter in their hands. She was anxious to finish her surgery on time because she was due to meet the asthma consultant at the school at lunchtime to give a talk to the pupils.

With her conviction that she had at least one of her problems under control, Callie was able to concentrate fully on her patients, and then later on the talk with the pupils. The consultant was clear and direct in his speech, leaving no room for doubt in the minds of the pupils that asthma inhalers did not make you fat and just how important it was to follow the regimen prescribed. There were a few questions at the end, but in general it seemed that the lecture, as well as the experiences of the young girls who had ended up in hospital, might have convinced them. And Callie sincerely hoped she had cut off their supply of illicit medication, well, Callie, the police and the headmistress between them.

Having the rest of the afternoon off, Callie decided on some therapeutic shopping, or rather window shopping, and not at the usual sorts of places she would visit. Miller had called to say that the Chief Super had refused his request to set up a sting operation, so she felt she had little choice but to try and do something herself.

She wandered the back streets of Hastings, looking for small, independent shops that sold cigarettes, and she found that there were an awful lot of them. With the stock all kept in display cabinets that had been screened so that you couldn't actually see what was in them, customers had to ask for the brand of their choice. Callie had no choice but to go in each of them and ask for the brand which had been targeted by the counterfeiters. In all of the shops, they handed her legitimate packs and she was forced to then ask if they had the "cheaper ones, in the dark green packs". Most of the shopkeepers looked at her blankly, some suspiciously, but no one brought out any of the counterfeit packs.

She was about to give up, feeling that she had wasted enough of her precious free afternoon already and perhaps her time would be better spent with a browse round some of her favourite shops in the Old Town, when she came across a rundown corner shop in a part of the town known as Bohemia that could possibly fit the bill.

The faded toys and adverts in the window looked to have been there for decades and the cards advertising things for sale and appeals for lost cats were curled and outnumbered by dead flies.

Callie pushed open the door and entered the shop. The smell of stale tobacco hit her immediately.

Inside, goods were stacked chaotically and shoppers were in constant danger of knocking over the boxes of crisps and fizzy pop that partially blocked the aisles. Trying to look like this was the sort of shop she frequented on a regular basis, Callie wandered around, picking her way carefully round the obstructions and collecting a few random purchases: a packet of biscuits, a tin of beans and some tissues. She surreptitiously wiped the worst of the dust off them before heading to the till. The man standing there, watching her every move, was as old and decrepit as the shop and as he went to ring up her purchases, Callie could see his fingers were heavily nicotine-stained.

She asked for the cigarettes and he turned to the secure cabinet behind him, bringing out the by now easily recognisable brand.

"I don't suppose you do the cheaper ones? In the dark green pack?" she asked, and was surprised when he not only didn't say no, but silently reached under the counter and pulled out a carton.

"Not sold in single packs," he said in broken English. "Two hundred only."

Callie nodded her agreement and held out her debit card.

"Cash," he said with barely disguised contempt.

With no real idea of how much money was expected, Callie held out some notes and waited while the man gave her some change. With the carton of cigarettes in her hand she hurriedly turned and went to the door, feeling him watch her every step of the way.

Once out of the shop, Callie made a mental note of its name and street number and then hurried round the corner where she stopped to catch her breath. Something about the whole experience had spooked her, and she felt grubby. She would need to shower to get rid of the tobacco smell, she was sure.

So now Callie knew the shop was being used by Claybourne for distribution, or one of them, anyway, the question was: who should she tell? If she was right and someone in Trading Standards had tipped him off about the last raid, there was no point in going to them with this information. But it was their investigation, the police were not about to interfere, given that they had more important things on their plate.

Callie remembered that Lisa Furnow had mentioned a boyfriend in the council. Now that she felt more able to trust her, Callie called and explained her predicament and was delighted to hear that Lisa's boyfriend didn't just work for the council, he was in Trading Standards. Of course, that meant that Lisa's boyfriend might be the source of the leak, but she thought that Lisa wouldn't go out with him if there was any chance of that being the case. Not when the subject that benefitted from the leak was Claybourne, but perhaps it would help her make up her mind if she met him. And anyway, she had no other choice, all she could do was hope that he wasn't the leak. Nothing ventured, nothing gained.

* * *

They met in a large anonymous chain pub on the outskirts of the town where they all hoped that no one they knew would be there to recognise them. Callie was pleased to see that the bright and cheerful family bar was almost empty when she entered. She ordered herself a fizzy water with ice and a slice, and took it to a table nicely tucked away in a corner. She had put the cigarettes in a carrier bag and tucked that under the table, out of the way.

The last vestiges of concern that Callie might have had about Lisa being involved with the FNM were dispersed when she came into the pub and Callie saw the photographer's boyfriend. He was black. There was no way she could be involved with a group like that and have a black boyfriend. They would not have tolerated it, and Callie couldn't believe her boyfriend would encourage it either. Callie was prepared to believe she was at the rally purely and simply to try and get something on Claybourne.

The couple spotted her at her corner table and brought their drinks over.

"This is Phil, Dr Hughes," Lisa introduced him.

"Callie, please," Callie corrected her and held out her hand.

"Lisa explained your concerns," Phil said and Callie hoped he wasn't going to be hard to convince of a possible leak in his department.

"And do you think it's possible?" she asked him.

He looked over at Lisa who nodded her encouragement and then turned back to Callie.

"It's something I've been concerned about for a while," he admitted. "But the abortive raid on the shop means it is even more likely."

"Oh." Callie hadn't expected it to be so easy. "Do you have any idea who the informer is?"

Phil looked embarrassed.

"Oh, come on, Phil, it's common knowledge that Claybourne's nephew works in the department," Lisa chipped in, helping him out.

That explained everything as far as Callie was concerned, and Lisa also, but Phil seemed less sure.

"I know you want it to be him, Lisa, but we have no proof."

"Well, maybe it's about time we did," Callie told him.

"What exactly did you have in mind?" he asked.

"I think we, you, should set up a sting operation to find out," Callie explained, and was pleased to see that he didn't object straight away.

"It's not that easy."

"I'm sure, but if it helps, I bought these in the corner shop on Bohemia Road this afternoon."

She pushed the carrier bag towards him with her foot, and he took it and glanced inside.

"You could say that you have information that the shop is being used to sell the cigarettes and set up a raid on the shop, just as you would be expected to do, and make sure Claybourne's nephew is aware of it," she continued.

"But—?"

"Already have surveillance in place, so that you catch them shifting the stock before the raid."

"And make sure he doesn't know about that." Lisa was smiling, she clearly liked the idea, but it wasn't her who Callie had to persuade.

Phil played with his drink as he gave the idea some thought.

"Is there anyone in the department you feel you could trust to do this with you?" she asked.

"My boss," he confirmed. "We discussed doing something like this, unofficially, when the last raid was a washout."

"And you think he'll go for it?"

"Of course, he will." Lisa was enthusiastic.

"It's possible." Phil was more cautious and Callie liked him all the more for that.

"But you will put it to him?"

He nodded.

"There are a lot of aspects we will have to work out, so I can't promise if, let alone when, it will happen, and I won't be able to tell you in advance, you do understand that, don't you?" He looked at Lisa as well, including her in the question and she nodded.

"Of course." Callie smiled at him.

"We'll just have to wait to read all about it in the papers." Lisa held up her drink. "Cheers."

They clinked glasses and Callie was more than a little pleased with the outcome. She just hoped they found something to definitively link Claybourne to the smuggling. Like Lisa, she would look forward to reading about his arrest in the papers, and hoped that it was in the not too distant future.

Chapter 29

Feeling pleased with herself that a second area of concern in her life was now on its way to resolution, thanks to her interference – as she had no doubt Miller would describe it – Callie decided to drop into the police station on her way home. She wanted to see how the response to the call for information about the age-regressed photo of body number nine was going. When she went into the incident room, she could see immediately, to her surprise, that there was a name written next to the photograph.

"Daniel Spencer," she said thoughtfully, going up to the board and touching the photo gently.

"Yup." Jayne Hales came and stood next to her. They both sighed as they looked at the photo. "Ran away from a children's home when he was thirteen. Mum was already dead of a heroin overdose, no one knew who Dad was. His gran's been trying to find him for years and had pretty much given up hope. She's dying of cancer."

As before, Callie felt pleased that the body had finally been identified, but sad for the poor woman who now knew that he was dead. Would it be a relief to know?

"She said, bad as it was to hear he was dead, she could die in peace, knowing there was nothing more she could

194

do for him." Jayne seemed to know what she had been thinking.

"Oh wow! That's just so awful. Does anyone know where he has been since he ran away?"

"We're getting some information in. It seems, like Michelle, that he went to London. Like most of them do. The Met Police are looking into that end. Now they have a name, they can track social security information, and The Sally Army are helping. They'll know more by the end of today, almost certainly."

Callie knew that The Salvation Army did a lot of work with runaways and the homeless, so they might, indeed, be able to cast light on where the two had been living, and what they had been doing to support themselves, although Callie had a pretty good idea about what they might have been doing.

"Did they show any signs of having been sex-workers or addicts? On the PM report?" she asked and wasn't surprised when Jayne nodded.

"They were both positive for a number of recreational drugs, although Michelle wasn't for ketamine, just Daniel, and yes, both had signs of regular and sometimes rough, sexual activity. Anal scarring was present in both cases, but no DNA or signs of recent sex. As you know, there's absolutely no chance of getting any information out of the GUM clinics, where they were probably treated for STDs or had HIV tests."

Callie knew Jayne was right, genito-urinary medicine clinics that treated patients for sexually transmitted diseases, would never reveal any details, always supposing the names and addresses their patients gave them weren't real anyway.

"And no idea what they were doing in Hastings?" she asked, although she knew that might never be known.

"Well, Michelle obviously came looking for Daniel, but what he was doing round here, we have no idea. Meeting a dealer perhaps?"

"You'd have thought there were plenty of those in London without having to come down here."

"Agreed, but why else?"

They both stared again at the photo and thought about a little boy lost.

* * *

It was a subject that Callie gave considerably more thought to that evening and later she discussed it with Billy.

"Why would Daniel, a rent boy and drug user or possible dealer, from London, be in Hastings?" she asked him.

He shrugged. "You don't need me to tell you that Hastings has a drug problem."

"But it's not, as far as I know, a centre for distribution. So, what could he possibly have been doing to get himself killed and dumped at sea?"

"Meeting someone? A friend?"

"Then they should have come forward, surely? When he didn't show up? Or when his picture was all over the local news?"

"Perhaps the friend was the killer."

Billy didn't seem that interested, but the more she thought about it, the more she thought that he was right. It made sense. Daniel came down from London to meet someone, or confront them, and that person killed him.

Michelle must have known he was coming down, and that he should have come back, which was why she was going round looking for him.

Or perhaps he often came down here? Had a regular client? Someone he had met in London but also had a place in the town. Or who had moved here. There were lots of people who had moved to Hastings from London and there were a number of derogatory names for them. There was the Down from London (DFL) brigade, often weekenders, putting up house prices but also spending their money in the town. And the FILTH, Failed in London, Try Hastings, as the displaced and disgruntled locals tended to call them. Daniel could have come to see any one of them, but it was in one of those groups that they would find his killer, and Michelle's killer; of that, Callie was sure. The question was, how could she, or the police narrow it down?

Chapter 30

Mid-morning, as Callie took a quick break to make herself a cup of coffee, she got a phone call from the principal of the academy asking if she would be willing to give some more talks to the pupils.

"You rated very highly in our feedback session," the principal told her, trying to butter her up. "You and the consultant both did, but we thought you would be a great addition to our regular speakers."

"Thank you, yes, of course." Flattered as she was, Callie wasn't quite able to make herself sound enthusiastic. "Erm, talks on anything in particular?"

"We have regular healthy lifestyle sessions with the younger pupils, and I am sure you would have plenty to say there, but I also thought you might like to talk to the older ones about being a GP. Inspire the girls to think about medicine as a career."

And so it was that Callie found herself agreeing to give talks two or three times a year, dates to be arranged.

Once she had put the phone down, she found herself instantly regretting the decision, wasn't her life busy enough? But it was too late to back out now. She took a sip of coffee and gave herself a mini-lecture on learning to say no before calling in the next patient on her list.

At the end of the session, she was surprised to see Miller sitting in the waiting room waiting for her.

"You should have asked them to let me know you were here," she said as she ushered him into her consulting room. "I would have fitted you in."

"Your receptionist said you were on your last patient, so I knew you wouldn't be long," he explained, as he sat in the patient's chair.

"How can I help?" she asked him.

He wriggled uncomfortably in his seat for a moment, clearly unsure that he was doing the right thing in confiding in her.

"Come on, out with it. I don't bite." She encouraged him with a smile and was pleased to see him reciprocate.

"The Met have found where our two victims lived. It's a council flat that's been sublet illegally and is only meant for two people, but actually about eight seem to have been living there. Daniel and Michelle had been friends a long time. Best friends, but not boyfriend and girlfriend."

"If they were both on the game, a sexual partner might not have been what they were looking for."

Miller nodded.

"And did they find out anything interesting from the others who lived in the flat?" she asked.

"Not really. To say that the occupants were uncooperative would be an understatement. They did manage to find a number of people who knew them, but most of them could not be said to be on good terms with the police, let's say."

"So, they haven't found out anything useful?" Callie couldn't hide her disappointment.

"Yes, and no. Most of them had no idea Daniel and Michelle were dead, it seems. There was no TV in the flat and they're not likely to be newspaper readers."

"And even if they did see their photos and an appeal for information, they probably would think it was because they were wanted for something, not that they were dead."

"Exactly, but once they knew both of them were dead, it did change things, for some of them at least, and they were willing to talk. It seems that Daniel had been telling everyone that he was onto a nice little earner. He'd seen a picture of one of his regular clients on the front page of a newspaper."

"And was planning a spot of blackmail."

"Well, they said he saw it as a reason to put his prices up."

"But if the client refused?"

"He might find himself talking to a journalist."

"That is definitely blackmail in my book." Callie thought for a moment. "Did they know who this client was?"

"No, unfortunately no one is admitting to being one of the boys that Daniel took with him when he went to meet this particular john."

"More than one?"

"Yes. It seems the client often liked more than two or three of them to go along at a time, so he could watch as well as join in, have a bit of a sex and drugs orgy."

"He sounds a right charmer."

"Mmm, it's not that uncommon, apparently, but not cheap either. The Met have the boys, some of whom are barely legal, I might add, looking at photographs in the hope someone can identify the man, but it's not looking hopeful."

"Well if they never met him—"

Miller looked at her as if she was being naive.

"I just hope none of them are planning on carrying on where Daniel left off," he told her.

Callie could understand his worry. If the man had been willing to kill twice to protect his secret, he wouldn't hesitate to do it again.

"I certainly hope they find out who it is quickly, but why the visit to me?"

Miller cleared his throat.

"We know this client must have a place in London, as that is where Daniel and his mates went for the parties," he told her. "And we've been investigating anyone who has homes both in London and down here."

"Makes sense. If he was coming down here to confront his client, there must be some connection."

"Exactly," he said. "There aren't that many people who live here, have a place in London as well and who might find it embarrassing if it came out they were having sex and drug parties with young men. We're trying to find out more about all of them, without ruffling any feathers. I could do without any more complaints to the Superintendent."

"I'm sure. You think it's a businessman, or someone like that? A family man, maybe, or a religious leader?"

"Yes." He hesitated. "Or an MP?"

"Oh!" Callie suddenly realised how well he fitted the description. "Ted Savage."

"Yes. Our local MP has a house at Pett Level. It's on the security register, in case it's attacked by terrorists or nutters."

Pett Level was where the migrants first came to shore, and was close to where both body number nine, or Daniel as she now knew him to be, and Michelle had been found. It all fitted so well.

"Does he have a boat?" she asked.

"We don't know. He lives on the beach, though, so it would seem likely. That's why I'm here, I wondered if you might know, seeing as you are such good buddies."

"Buddies? I hardly know the man."

"That's not what Councillor Claybourne says. He says you and Mr Savage are 'close friends'." Miller did the irritating bunny ears gesture as he said the words.

"Judging by what you've told me, if he is our man, I'm the wrong sex for that."

"Maybe Claybourne doesn't know that."

"No. I can't imagine him keeping quiet about it if he did. Have there been any rumours about Savage's sexuality?"

Callie firmly believed that such matters were entirely personal, but the tabloid press disagreed and if there had been any hint, she would have expected them to pick up on it.

"No. And the MP does of course have a wife, which might put people off the scent."

Callie gave that some thought and realised that it fitted quite well with her impression of Mrs Savage as more an assistant or manager than a partner.

"Anyway, I have no idea if Ted, Mr Savage, has a boat or not. I've not been to his home and I didn't even know he had a house at Pett Level."

"That's a shame." Miller was disappointed.

"And I've no idea about his sexuality, contrary to Claybourne's insinuations," she added for good measure. "Can't you just ask him? About the boat, that is."

"I may have to, but at the moment I want to keep it low key. I don't have enough to get a warrant, for anyone on my short list of possible suspects, let alone an MP. I'm just going to have to wait and see if they manage to get anything more definite in London." He didn't seem all that hopeful.

After he had left, Callie gave it some more thought. She had no reason to visit Savage at his home, but she could drop into his surgery, after all, he had invited her. She could ask him about a boat, perhaps invent a love of sailing, fishing or some such, so long as he didn't actually invite her out on it. She couldn't actually go with him anyway, she told herself, not when he might have used the boat to dispose of two bodies. That would be both dangerous and silly, particularly as she was so prone to

202

seasickness. He'd know immediately that she wasn't really keen on sailing if she was leaning over the side throwing up the whole trip.

* * *

When Callie got to the MP's office building, she had half-expected to find no one there. The politician's routine surgery wasn't meant to start for another hour and she had hoped to find Mrs Savage alone, preparing for it. The red car was certainly there, but she was surprised to see workmen busy carrying in boxes of carpet tiles from a panel van parked nearby.

She almost bumped into one of the men hurrying out of the door as she went to enter the building.

"Can't go in there, love," he told her. "Just laying the new floor and we have to get it finished before they open later this afternoon."

She stood at the door and looked in. The smell of new paint and other chemicals used in the refurbishment, struck her immediately.

The walls were now an elegant dove grey and darker grey carpet tiles were being laid along the short corridor. She could see the theme continued into the waiting room and she leaned in to get a better look inside. A quick glance to her left suggested that even the little kitchenette hadn't escaped the decorating with a shiny new vinyl floor. It looked as though the entire office suite had been given a complete make-over.

"We're not open yet. You'll have to come back later."

Callie jumped back guiltily and turned to face Mrs Savage. She was dressed in her usual style, cream cotton shirt, dark blue skirt, pearl stud earrings, and flat blue pumps; plain and understated, very professional, nothing flashy. Nothing to get her noticed at all.

"Dr Hughes!" The MP's wife couldn't hide her surprise, or her disapproval at seeing Callie. "What are you doing here?"

"I, um, wanted a word with Ted, about the migrants." Callie smiled and tried to look innocent, taken aback by the rudeness. "I didn't realise you were planning to redecorate." She indicated inside and moved back as another workman hurried in with more carpet tiles.

"You must have seen how tired and grubby it was, when you came before."

"Well, yes," Callie agreed, she had noticed it, but she couldn't help feeling the timing of this refurbishment was suspicious.

Mrs Savage looked at her watch pointedly and spoke to the carpet tile layer on his knees in the corridor.

"You have fifteen minutes to finish."

She got nothing but a grunt in reply as the man carried on working. Callie thought the woman looked stressed; perhaps the fact that the workmen were behind and the office might not be ready for when the constituents arrived was enough to cause it.

"Ted is running a bit late, so he won't have time to talk to you."

"Oh, right, well, I'll drop in another day, perhaps. Thank you." Callie started towards her car.

"A word of advice, Dr Hughes?"

Callie turned back.

"My husband flirts with everybody. It's just the way he is. It doesn't make you something special."

Callie could feel a blush rising up her neck at this put-down, but Mrs Savage had already turned back to oversee the workmen.

* * *

"You must see that the timing is a bit coincidental, to put it mildly," Callie told Miller. She had rushed to see him as soon as she had left the MP's office to tell him about the decorators.

Jeffries didn't seem convinced.

"Yes, but that's exactly what it could be, Doc, a coincidence. Could have been planned months ago."

"Well, that's something you could check, isn't it?" She tried to conceal her irritation, but failed.

"Given that the bodies were found on the beach, I was more interested in his house than the office," Miller added.

"Yes, but they could have been moved. If they were killed in the office, he could have taken them to his house or wherever he keeps his boat."

"If he has a boat."

"He's trying to cover up the evidence. Why else would he redecorate now?" Callie was more than a little exasperated, she had been so sure they would be interested.

"If he's the killer, and that's a big if."

"And even if he is getting rid of the forensic evidence, he's done it, hasn't he? We're too late," Jeffries chipped in.

"But you could get hold of the carpet tiles before they're dumped. If you are quick enough."

Miller did at least seem to consider this.

"I took down the name and phone number of the company doing the work. It was on the van."

She held out her phone to show him the photograph she had taken of it before leaving. Miller ignored it.

"Look, have you got any other people who fit the bill?" she pushed him. "You seemed pretty sure it was him."

"We've got about twenty on the list." Jeffries was still openly dismissive. "And much as I have a low opinion of politicians—"

"Very low," Miller chipped in.

"Like Councillor Claybourne, I have a hard time thinking of him as a murderer," Jeffries continued.

"Are any of these other suspects really viable?" Callie wasn't about to give up, not just yet.

"None as good as Savage," Miller conceded. He was thoughtful. "I just don't see how I can get a warrant on the evidence I have."

"Do you need one for a carpet that's been taken away? Can't you check with the CPS? I mean, Michelle Carlisle had a head injury, what if it happened there? In his office? He could be getting rid of the flooring because of a blood stain."

"Or he could just be redecorating." Jeffries clearly wasn't convinced.

"If you don't move to get the discarded carpet tiles now, before they go to the tip or are destroyed in some way, it will be too late, or will involve sifting through tons of rubbish."

Miller could see the sense in this argument and he certainly wouldn't want the cost of having to pay for a large-scale search of the council landfill site at a later date if Callie was proved right, but still he hesitated.

"I take it none of Daniel's friends have identified Savage as the client?" Callie really wasn't going to let it rest.

"No, that would be too easy." Miller washed his face with his hands as he thought about what he could do. Callie crossed her fingers and willed him to agree to it.

"Sod it," he said and reached for the phone.

Chapter 31

Callie was on tenterhooks as she waited at home to hear the result of Miller's phone call. Or phone calls. When she had finally given up and left the incident room, he was still trying to persuade the CPS that he had enough cause for a warrant to seize the discarded carpet. They clearly did not agree, and she understood that, but meanwhile, the evidence, if there was any, could have been lost. She just hoped Miller got permission to prevent the carpet's destruction, even if they weren't allowed to actually take it away or examine it for evidence at this point. What always seemed so easy in television dramas, was clearly not so in real life. Miller's argument that the carpet had already been discarded and was therefore no longer the property of the MP, seemed logical to Callie but she knew the CPS and the Superintendent both needed to give their blessing to any action, and then Miller also had to persuade the company to hand it over, which they could quite rightly refuse to do, if he didn't have a warrant.

She finally got a quick phone call from Jayne to tell her the outcome at seven o'clock in the evening.

"Hi, Doc, thought you might want to know what was going on."

That was an understatement.

"A couple of us went to the firm and found out that the rubbish from the job was still in the back of the van, thank goodness. They were just about to take it to the landfill site. There was a bit of a wrangle about stopping them. The warrant hadn't come through, they wanted to do it straight away because they needed the van first thing, yada, yada, yada."

"But you managed to stop them?"

"Yes, eventually they agreed to unload it into a pile at the back of their yard and we covered it with a tarpaulin, while we wait to find out if we can take it."

"You mean it's still there?"

"Yup."

"Is anyone guarding it?"

"No, but the yard is locked and covered by CCTV. I think we've put the fear of God into them enough to ensure they don't do anything stupid while we wait for the powers that be to pull their collective fingers out."

"Do you reckon you'll get a warrant?"

Jayne hesitated before answering.

"It's not looking hopeful, if I'm honest. It's not like we have any evidence linking your man with the crimes. I think the boss is just hoping we turn something up that gives us grounds for one."

Callie chose to ignore the "your man" comment. It just made her even more angry about the lies Claybourne was spreading, apparently very successfully.

"Meanwhile, the carpet is lying in a yard, and any evidence on it gets degraded?"

"Yes." Jayne didn't sound any happier than Callie did at the situation. "But less so than if it was at the tip, at least it's under a tarpaulin and we will just have to hope it doesn't rain too much, or overheats, or—"

"Gets eaten by rats," Callie interrupted.

"Indeed. I hadn't thought of that one, but you're right, I will have to add rats to my list of worries now."

Callie thanked Jayne for letting her know the situation, frustrating as it was.

* * *

Next morning, Callie got a text from Lisa, telling her to watch the local news on television and that it would make her very happy. Callie hurriedly switched it on, as she made herself tea and toast for breakfast.

She had to wait a frustrating few minutes listening to lots of celebrity gossip before the news headlines came on and, sure enough, it did make her happy.

The picture changed to the street outside the council offices.

"This morning, there were simultaneous raids on a shop thought to be suspected of selling illegal cigarettes and also the home and offices of a local councillor."

The picture changed to a large detached house where two or three men could be seen carrying boxes out of the garage and placing them in a van.

"A large number of items have been seized at the shop and home of the local councillor, and we understand he is now being questioned in relation to suspected avoidance of duty, selling contraband goods, and a number of other charges."

Callie felt like cheering. If he had boxes of cigarettes stored at his home, there was no way he would get away completely clean, which should put paid to his fledgling political career. If Claybourne had only known he didn't really need to try and goad Savage, and Callie, he might have got away with it, at least for a while longer, but she was delighted that she had managed to play a part in his downfall, however small.

The next item on the local news was less pleasing. Pictures of a fire at a builders' yard.

"The fire started in a pile of rubbish in a corner of the Truman's site and fortunately the fire services were able to extinguish the blaze before it spread to nearby offices," the presenter said and Callie watched as she saw a man she knew to be the fire investigator kicking over the few, still smoking remains of the carpet tiles from Ted Savage's constituency office.

Chapter 32

Miller was in his office with the fire investigator, Chris Butterworth, when Callie marched into the incident room. Callie knew Butterworth from an arson case he had worked in the past and she was pleased to see that he was there, and already on this case.

Miller moved back slightly, preparing himself for the onslaught she had prepared all the way to see him, and held up a hand to stop her launching into her complaint.

"I know, I know!" he said quickly. "We should have got the carpet out of there before this happened."

"Or at least posted someone outside the yard."

"I organised extra patrols but didn't have the resources for a twenty-four-hour guard." He stopped. It was clear this wasn't going to wash with Callie. To say she was angry was very much an understatement. "The good news is that it does raise our level of suspicion," he added lamely.

"Even if it lowers your level of available evidence," she hissed. "Did Savage know you had stopped the firm from disposing of the carpet?"

"Not as far as we know. The owner denies telling him, but any one of the workers could have said something, and the yard is easily visible from the road."

Butterworth cleared his throat and she turned to hear what he had to say.

"There was a positive reading for accelerant at the site, so we know the fire was probably started deliberately."

"Of course, it was started deliberately!" She was fuming. "Carpets don't spontaneously catch fire." She knew she was being unfair. "Sorry," she said and Butterworth smiled.

"It's okay, I know how it feels when all the evidence goes up in flames."

It was, after all, his job.

"Was there anything left that could be tested for DNA?"

Butterworth shook his head.

"I very much doubt it." He shrugged as he explained, "The heat, the accelerant—" He didn't really need to say more. Callie knew that they would almost certainly have destroyed any DNA between them.

"CCTV?" she asked hopefully.

"Spray paint." Again, Butterworth didn't need to say more.

"Brilliant." Callie looked as unhappy as the two men at this.

* * *

"I mean, it really makes me cross."

Callie was still fuming as she spoke to Kate on the phone later.

"I'm getting that message."

"All they needed to do was have someone outside the yard in a patrol car."

"Policemen don't grow on trees, Callie," Kate replied. "Look, I know it's frustrating, but look at it this way, it makes the case so much stronger against Savage. At least in the minds of the police and it will make the CPS more likely to listen, too. All Miller needs to do is concentrate on getting the evidence."

"What evidence is left?" Callie asked. "I mean, if the murders were committed in the office, any forensics have long gone now."

"The bodies would have to have been transported elsewhere. I am sure Miller will be applying for warrants on the Savages' cars, and trying to find out if they have a boat and going for that, too."

Callie knew she was right, but the CPS's caution over the warrant for the discarded carpet left her concerned that they still wouldn't listen and be equally cautious about giving Miller any kind of a warrant for the vehicles. If the Met didn't find any connection between Savage and the two victims, what possible evidence did Miller have that could convince them? Nothing! He didn't even know if Savage owned a boat.

Callie spent some time researching the politician online. It was amazing how much you could glean from old interviews, tweets and other social media sources, but to find it and put it all together would take more time and probably more skills than she had. She found an interview with him in his "Hastings home" and could see that there were sea views out of the window. She knew the house was in Pett Level because Miller had told her that, and it was a small enough village for her to feel fairly confident that she could wander round and maybe spot the most likely place, or the MP's car on the drive.

She thought back to the visits she had made to the office and to the meeting at the leisure centre. There had definitely not been any big important cars, the sort of cars you might expect powerful men to drive. Nothing that she could say she would recognise. Just the immaculate red hatchback, possibly Mrs Savage's car, she thought, or just the run-around they used when they were in Hastings. Perhaps she would see that.

She grabbed her own car keys and a jacket and headed out the door.

* * *

It was just beginning to get dark when she arrived in the small village where the Savage constituency home was located. She parked on the road, with a sad look at the pub carpark. It had barriers now that the pub was shut, and there were weeds growing through the tarmac, it wouldn't be long before nature claimed it back completely if the pub remained empty. She knew there were plans for it to become a doctors' surgery and café, a real community hub for the locals, and she hoped it went forward soon even if she was still sad that a pub she had frequented in her youth had gone. The Smugglers had been her meeting place of choice when she needed to be sure she wouldn't bump into anyone her parents knew and who might let drop that she was underage to be drinking alcohol. She turned away from the derelict pub and looked along the road towards the row of coastguard cottages and the houses beyond. To her right was the way over the bank to the shingle beach and the slipway for launching the independent rescue boat, whose volunteers covered the area and helped when swimmers and small boats got into trouble off the beach. They had been the ones to find the migrant boat, upturned and empty apart from one poor man who had thought to keep safe by tying himself to the side of the boat. With a shudder she remembered how battered his body had been when she pronounced him dead.

Callie walked up the path to the top of the bank which separated the houses from the sea. It was about ten foot higher than the road and designed to protect the homes from storm tides. There was a path leading towards the cliffs and Fairlight Glen, the route she had taken when the bodies were washed up there. It was almost completely dark, but when she turned, the wide, concrete walkway along the top of the bank and behind the houses was brighter, illuminated by the light spilling from the homes. There was a gate to stop cars using the walkway except when they had a key. There were boats at the top of the shingle shelf and the path was presumably used to tow them to the slipway when needed.

Callie went around the gate, which was only designed to prevent vehicular access, not pedestrians. With the sea to her right, she walked along the back of the houses, which were all about ten feet lower than the path she was on. Most had stairs, with locked gates at the top, leading up from their small gardens to the path where she was standing. Moving forward, she could see that the older coastguard cottages had no sea view from the ground floor because of the bank, but at least some of the newer houses were built with bedrooms or utility rooms on the ground floor and living areas higher up to take advantage of the spectacular scenery. Their owners' desire to have open and unfettered views also meant that she could see right into many of them, although the rooms seemed mostly empty.

As she walked along the path, she could see into one where a couple were having pre-dinner drinks, the man standing behind the counter of the open plan kitchen, stirring a pot whilst the woman flicked through a magazine in the seating area. Neither were aware of her standing on the path, looking in and Callie thought that she would hate being on public show like they were. She understood the need for net curtains, even if she didn't like their look. She would be tempted to put in tinted glass, making it impossible to see in, if she owned one of these houses. Not that she would ever be able to afford one, she thought, even if she wanted to. Many were weekend getaways for city folk and although some had lamps on, Callie suspected most were empty midweek and the lights were to deter burglars rather than an indication that the houses were occupied.

The one picture Callie had found of the MP at his home, showed him in a large, minimalist, open plan "living space" as the gushing interviewer had described it. There was no way the photo had been taken in a small cottage, so she hurried past them to the larger houses beyond. Her problem was, there were several, large, white, modern, box-like, houses along the beachfront. She moved on to inspect the next brightly lit, minimalist white blockhouse, in which every perfectly neat and tidy room appeared empty of emotion as well as people. It was one of these larger and flashier houses that Callie felt sure belonged to the MP and his wife-slash-secretary. One of the facts Callie had managed to find out was that Mrs Savage had indeed been his secretary before marrying him and continuing her work for the MP but with a slightly elevated status.

Slowly, she walked the length of the houses but saw nothing to tell her which house was owned by the MP. Callie had noted several boats, pulled up on the shore, but none looked as if they had been used recently. She also realised that the noise involved in moving a boat from the shingle would mean that it would be likely to attract attention. She stopped at the last house, where a spaniel barked at her through the closed window, suggesting that this one was occupied, even if the home owners were sensibly hidden somewhere in a room not on show to the world, or at least that they would be back at some point to feed the dog.

Callie turned back; the path went on, along the top of the bank, but there were no more houses for her to look into.

She walked back to the slipway, still looking into any of the houses that she could see into in the hope that she would recognise one from the picture of the MP's home. But there was nothing and no one, just the couple she had seen before, now seated at the dining table, eating whatever the man had cooked.

At the slipway, she walked down its short length to the end where it became nothing more than shingle. The tide was out and it would be a long, tiring and noisy job to try and launch a boat here at any time other than high tide. Callie couldn't believe that Ted Savage could have manhandled a boat, and bodies, to the sea, not once, but twice without attracting attention. Not from here, anyway.

Feeling a little deflated that her theory on how the murderer got rid of the bodies really wasn't working out, Callie went back down to the road and walked along the unpaved and poorly lit street, wanting to see the entrances to the buildings she had just walked past on the other side. Perhaps she would at least be able to identify the MP's home from the road if she saw the car. First, she walked past the coastguard cottages, a terrace of well-kept homes with pretty gardens. Keeping as close to their front walls as possible, listening for traffic and looking for headlights that might mean she needed to get out of the way, she made her way forward. Beyond the cottages were the larger, more modern buildings.

Trying not to look suspicious, because the last thing she wanted was for some nosy-parker neighbour calling the police, Callie looked into the front driveways of all of the houses. Some had garages, double garages even, despite the lack of space between the road and the main entrances, and they could have had cars inside them, but Callie quickly realised that the houses that really were occupied, rather than empty and waiting for their owners to visit, usually had the cars parked outside, not in the garages. Probably because manoeuvring the vehicles in and out was difficult in the confined space.

As she moved onto the next house, Callie saw a small red car that she was sure was the one she had seen at the office and at the meeting where she had met Ted Savage. It was, indeed, parked outside a white minimalist cube of a house. There wasn't another car outside, which perhaps meant that Teresa Savage was home alone and that her husband was in their London flat. Callie stood and thought about what she should do next. There was a garage that might hold another car, or a boat, but if she went up close enough to look through the small window, she worried she might trigger motion sensors or some other security device. Not so bad, if that was just lights, but if there was a more sophisticated system that involved alarms inside the house as well, or even CCTV, she could be in trouble. He was an MP, after all, she should expect a high level of security.

Meanwhile, she recognised that standing in the road, suspiciously staring up at the house wasn't without problems. Her mind was made up by the sudden appearance of headlights in the distance, she had only moments before she would be lit up in the car's beams. She moved swiftly into the driveway and slipped between the fence and the garage, crossing her fingers and holding her breath, frightened that any movement could set off an alarm.

She was out of luck, the light over the garage came on in response to her movement.

The car went by but Callie stayed where she was for a moment longer, listening for any alien sounds or signs that she had disturbed anyone. There was nothing but silence and then the sound of a door opening. A light over the front door to the house came on, throwing the whole area into brilliant white light and dark shadows. Callie's foot was in the light, but the rest of her was in shadow. Very carefully, Callie moved her foot slowly back and inched along the side of the garage, making sure that she was completely hidden from view, then she stopped and held her breath again, as she listened. She heard footsteps come to the garage door and rattle it, checking it was still locked, there was a pause, while the owner of the footsteps presumably also listened for sounds of someone in the shadows. Callie had an itchy nose and had to restrain herself from scratching it. She knew the itch didn't really exist, that it was purely psychological, but still the desire to scratch her nose or sneeze was almost over-powering. At last she heard the person move back towards the house, hopefully reassured that there was no one there, and after what seemed like an age, she heard the sound of the front door closing and she was able to breathe out.

After the fright of so nearly being caught she stayed where she was for a while, catching her breath and taking in her surroundings. She was in a narrow gap between the garage and the ivy-covered wall that marked the edge of the property. Behind her, and a little above, was a small narrow window into the back part of the garage. It was sealed shut, but with a bit of climbing up, using the wall and the garage itself for leverage, Callie was able to get herself into a position to look into the garage. Light was coming in from another window on the side nearest to the house, because the security lights had not yet clicked off. In that light she was able to see the usual detritus found in people's garages, and a small RIB on a trailer. Eureka!

Suddenly Callie herself was flooded in light, caught in the beam of a torch.

"Dr Hughes, this is a surprise," Teresa Savage said, as Callie lost her grip and slid down the garage wall.

Chapter 33

Held in the glare of the high-intensity torch beam, and with absolutely nowhere to hide, Callie sidled out of the space between the garage and the wall. She felt like an actor on a stage, or more appropriately, an escapee from prison, caught in the searchlight before she had even got to the main gate. As she inched her way out, she desperately tried to think up a reasonable explanation for why she was sneaking about the woman's home after dark, but for the life of her, she couldn't come up with one.

Teresa Savage looked her intruder up and down as Callie stood there trying to think what she should say. Something, anything, to explain away her presence, but she failed to come up with anything better than, "Hello, it's a surprisingly large garage, isn't it?"

Teresa Savage said nothing and Callie felt that the woman must think that she was completely mad.

"Why don't you come in, Dr Hughes," she said finally. "Then you can tell me why you were sneaking around my property in the dark."

Teresa Savage turned and walked towards the closed front door. She had presumably shut it to trick whoever was behind the garage into thinking she had gone back inside, and it had worked, Callie thought ruefully. It didn't seem to occur to Teresa Savage that Callie wouldn't follow her, and, surprising herself, Callie did. She knew the wise thing would be to refuse, plead a pressing engagement, an appointment with someone she was running late for, but the need to try and explain her way out of the situation, and her inherent good manners meant that she followed the woman into the house, closing the door behind her. Besides, she wanted to know if the woman knew her husband hosted orgies, and if she had any suspicions that he might be a killer.

Mrs Savage led the way up the stairs that were directly in front of the door, and into the open plan kitchen and living area. She went straight to the kettle, going through the ritual of making tea. It gave them both time to think.

"Do take a seat, Dr Hughes," she said as she busied herself with cups and tea bags. "How do you take it?"

"Milk, no sugar," Callie dutifully replied, taking a seat at the breakfast bar.

The situation was totally surreal, she thought. Would the MP's wife call the police? That would be the normal thing to do if you found someone on your property, looking through the windows, wouldn't it? Although the fact that they did know each other might complicate matters. They'd probably believe she was a stalker, which she supposed she was, in a way.

"Is Ted, your husband, in London?" Callie could feel herself panic slightly. Did she really think Mrs Savage wouldn't know that Ted was her husband? She felt an overwhelming urge to giggle, but managed to turn it into a cough and turned in her seat to look out of the window at the view of the sea, or at least where the view of the sea would be if it wasn't a dark and cloudy night, with not even a bit of moonlight reflecting off the water.

"Yes, he'll probably drive down later tonight after the sitting, or tomorrow, if it goes on too long."

Callie knew that Westminster business often went on late into the night, MPs were always complaining about it and how it was unduly hard on those with families. She turned back as Mrs Savage put a mug of tea down in front of her and stood facing Callie, staying on the other side of the breakfast bar.

"Now, Dr Hughes, perhaps you'd like to tell me exactly why you were sneaking around my garden at this time of night?" Her tone was still fairly light, faintly remonstrative as if she expected Callie to confess to a fetish about garages, or a crush on her husband.

Callie hesitated, playing with the mug before coming to the conclusion that the only course of action was to tell the truth, or, at least, the partial truth.

"I wanted to see if you had a boat."

"A boat?" Mrs Savage seemed surprised. "Well, we do, as a matter of fact."

"Yes."

"I don't think you will find many people living along here who don't."

"No, I don't suppose you would."

"And why did you particularly want to see if we had a boat?"

"Because, whoever killed Michelle Carlisle and Daniel Spencer, had to have access to a boat in order to dump their bodies at sea."

Mrs Savage vigorously stirred her drink, and took a sip. She hadn't been expecting that answer, Callie could tell.

"And you thought we might be involved?"

"I was trying to exclude Ted."

"And have you?"

"No. But perhaps you can help me there."

"I can certainly do that, because it's just ridiculous. Ted is a good man."

"Yes, I'm sure he is." Callie wasn't so sure, but she didn't want to antagonise the woman any more than she already had.

"Don't let your tea get cold," Mrs Savage said, nodding at the mug in front of Callie.

"Do you think it's possible that your husband might have known Daniel?" Callie asked as she sipped the drink, trying not to show her distaste as she realised that it had been sweetened. Perhaps Mrs Savage was more rattled than she seemed and had mixed up the two mugs.

"It's possible," she replied. "Ted knows a lot of people in London. He's a sociable man, you've seen that. He flirts with everyone. Men and women. People get the wrong idea."

"In what way?"

"They think he's interested in them when he isn't really." She gave Callie a look that suggested Callie was one of those people.

"Did you know he was gay?" Callie asked. She didn't honestly believe that his wife wouldn't know if he was, but it was always possible. She took another sip, once she had got over the shock at how sweet it was, she had to admit it was quite nice. Sugar was a treat she didn't often allow herself, so she had some more, she deserved it after the shock of being found behind the garage. Sweet tea for shock, that was what they said, didn't they?

"He isn't, strictly speaking. That would be too easy, too uncomplicated for Ted. He is attracted to people of either sex, or rather, both sexes," Mrs Savage continued. "I've always known that, but I loved him and wanted to try and make a go of it. I thought we would, for a while, despite his frequent infidelities." She seemed truly sad that it hadn't worked out as well as she had hoped.

"It must have been difficult."

"Yes. I knew he was seeing other people, of course, but I had no idea about the rent boys, or the drugs. I would have stopped it if I had known, you see, told him to stop destroying everything we had worked so hard to build. Then that boy turned up and tried to get money out of us."

Callie's eyes had begun to close, she was feeling so tired, but they opened with a jolt as she realised that Mrs Savage had known about the blackmail. Or had Callie just told her, she couldn't quite remember the conversation. What had she said?

"As if I would ever let a nobody like him ruin a good man's career. Ted was worth a hundred times more than that, that skinny streak of street scum," Mrs Savage continued. "I mean, I could cope with the other people, he could always come out of the closet, or confess to being a sex addict and if that was all it was, there would have been no danger, nothing to threaten us with. I could have put a positive spin on it, about him having the courage to come out, tell the truth. I could have been the understanding wife and helper, standing by him. We could still live together, even. But this!"

Callie was struggling to understand what she was saying, and her voice seemed to be coming from further away.

"Ted's failing is that he's just too trusting. He always wants to believe the best of people, to help them, even if they don't deserve it. He wanted to pay the boy off, thought that would be the end of it, can you believe it?"

Callie's eyes were closing again and she felt the tea slop onto her hand, she went to put the mug down, but missed the worktop. The mug smashed on the floor.

"I'm so sorry," she slurred and tried to get off the stool but found that her legs didn't seem to want to do what they were told. How embarrassing, to be drunk and incapable in this lovely house, she needed to get back to her own home. Mrs Savage didn't seem concerned, or even to have noticed the broken mug and spilled tea, she just carried on talking about stuff that Callie was having difficulty taking in.

"I couldn't let anyone stop Ted's career, could I? His work is just too important. Even if the person who was doing the destroying was Ted himself."

Callie realised she had been drugged; the taste disguised by the sugar. She was ridiculously pleased with herself for being able to work it out. The question now was, what was she going to do about it? She shook her head, trying to clear it, but it just made her dizzy and she had to hold on to the breakfast bar to stop herself from falling off the stool.

"The boy wasn't really a problem, I borrowed Ted's phone and invited him down for a party. Ted often had parties, always in London because it would be hard to keep it quiet in a small village like this."

Callie could believe it. Stopping the boys from making a noise, or running down the beach for a midnight skinny dip, would be difficult.

"The boy was surprised to be met at the station by me rather than Ted but once I'd told him I was taking him to our yacht where this supposed party was taking place, and that Ted would give him the money there, he was quite happy. Chatting away non-stop. I suspect he had taken a little something, some Dutch courage before facing Ted. Makes sense, don't you think?"

Callie was finding it hard to make sense of anything at all. She felt awful.

"Anyway, it all worked to my advantage and he went with me to the marina and got in my little boat no problem at all. How was he to know we don't have a yacht, just a little inflatable with an outboard." She laughed at the boy's silly mistake. "I gave him an alcopop I'd added a little extra something to, to get him in the party mood, I said. Ketamine really isn't that hard to get hold of, you know. My brother, well, he has his uses, let's say. Daniel didn't suspect anything was wrong with the drink, although it took quite a long time to work. How are you feeling, Dr Hughes?"

"Okay." Callie tried to smile, but she wasn't sure she had succeeded, she wasn't sure she had replied either, but Mrs Savage didn't seem to mind.

"He kept asking me how far it was, how long it would take to get there." She smiled sadly at the memory. "I had to say the boat was down the coast quite a way, he didn't know any better, didn't notice that we were going round in circles and then he fell asleep, just like I'd planned. Didn't stir when I took off some of his more distinctive clothes and jewellery. Put him in an old shirt and tied the remains of one of those useless life jackets that were washing up all along the coast around his waist." She paused, remembering how it had all happened. "It was a little harder to tip him over the side than I'd expected, and I had to hold him under using the paddle, until I was sure he was beyond saving, but it worked perfectly. Just one more body amongst all those others, until you started with your nasty little suspicions, suggesting he wasn't the same as them."

Callie found herself apologising, even though she wasn't quite sure what for; it was enough that this kind, capable woman was cross with her, wasn't it? Or was she kind? Kind people didn't drug and kill boys, did they? Callie couldn't think.

"The girl was more of a problem. I hadn't expected her to turn up at the constituency office. Should have realised the boy would have told someone where he was going, what he was doing."

Callie remembered the girl's head wound. They always bled a lot. That would explain the need to redecorate the office, burn the carpet.

"Why did he kill her?" Callie asked in a slurred voice – at least she thought she asked but Mrs Savage carried on talking, ignoring the question as she walked around the breakfast bar.

"There was a bit of a confrontation, I hadn't even realised I had picked up the kettle. I think I was going to suggest a cup of tea. Quite a mess. Good job my brother works at that building company, he was a great help, again. Made sure they came round to clean up nice and quick and then let me know when you made them keep hold of the carpet. Of course, I had to pay more, nearly double, and then more again for him to set fire to it all. He didn't know why the police were interested in it. I told him Ted had been accused of rape by some little tart, and that we needed to get rid of the carpet in case there was semen on it. You know, like Bill Clinton and that dress."

She was standing beside Callie now and put her arm round her, gently helping her off the stool. Callie was very grateful to her, because she certainly couldn't have managed it herself, for some reason, the room seemed to be moving in circles around her. It was hard to remain upright.

"Let me help you down the stairs, dear. You know they really are very steep."

Callie was having great difficulty placing one foot in front of the other. The stairs seemed a long way away. She felt as if everything was sliding away from her and the light kept fading in from the edges, not smoothly but in jagged little pieces. She had no idea what time of day it was or how long she had been there.

Suddenly there was the bang of a door closing and Mrs Savage froze for a moment.

"Hello?" A man's voice came up the stairs and Mrs Savage let go of Callie. Without her support, Callie slid slowly to the floor.

There was the sound of footsteps on the stairs and then Ted Savage was there.

"What the hell's going on, Teresa?"

"She knows."

"You said you had it all under control."

"I did, but I found her snooping round, looking for the boat."

Ted knelt down beside her and Callie struggled to focus on his face, so that she could understand what he was saying to her. She hoped it would help, because she hadn't got a clue what was going on, either.

"Are you all right, Dr Hughes?" he asked her solicitously. There was also more than a hint of anxiety in his voice, she thought. "Are you hurt?"

She tried to shake her head but that only made things worse.

"Drugged," she managed to say through thick lips. She hoped he understood what she was saying because she wasn't sure how clearly she was speaking and she didn't think she could manage to say it again. He nodded his understanding.

"We need to deal with her." Mrs Savage was taking charge again and Callie knew that was not a good thing. "Find her keys, they must be in her jacket pocket."

"No!"

Callie was surprised by the vehemence in his tone.

"We have to do it. She knows everything."

"I can't."

"You are so bloody useless!" Mrs Savage shouted at him and then bent down and started going though Callie's pockets, finding her keys quickly.

"Go and fetch her car and bring it to the front door." She handed the keys to Ted. "Now!" she ordered.

He moved towards the stairs but then stopped and stood there for a moment, doing nothing. Callie tried to will him to refuse.

"This isn't right," he said, weakly.

"You brought this on yourself," his wife said, "with your stupid self-destructive behaviour. Now you have to help me clear it up."

"I can't. It has to stop."

"You managed to help me get rid of the girl's body. This is no different. Now go and get the bloody car!"

But still he didn't move to do as she ordered.

"No. This is different."

"In what way?"

"She's alive, for God's sake."

"Well, if that's your only worry," she spat.

Mrs Savage went to the kitchen area and came back with a large, cast-iron frying pan. She headed over to where Callie was half-sitting half-lying near the top of the stairs, drawing back her weapon as she did so, preparing to strike. Callie tried to hold up an arm to protect herself but, she knew, even in her drugged state, that her arm would be useless to stop the blow, even if she did manage to raise it. There was nothing she could do to stop herself from being killed and she felt strangely calm about it.

"No!" Ted grabbed the pan and wrenched it out of his wife's grasp. "You can't, Teresa. I won't let you hurt anyone else. It has to stop."

She lunged at him, trying to get the pan from him and in the struggle to keep it, he pushed her away from him, a hard push, a deliberate push, and there was a surprised cry and the sound of someone tumbling, bumping down the stairs.

Ted stood there, frozen. An anguished expression on his face, frying pan in his hand, looking down towards the hallway.

Callie managed to get onto her hands and knees and crawl to where she could see. Mrs Savage lay in a crumpled heap, her head against the front door and her neck at an odd angle as a slowly expanding pool of blood formed under her head.

Ted Savage let out a whimper and dropped the pan, making Callie jump. He didn't go to his wife, but came and sat next to Callie, tears pouring down his face. She comforted him, as best she could, just by being there.

After what seemed an age, but was probably no more than ten minutes, Ted reached into his pocket and brought out his phone. To Callie's relief he called for the emergency services, because she was in no state to do it. Once she knew help was on its way, she closed her eyes and let sleep take over.

Chapter 34

Callie was sitting in the back of an ambulance, a blanket draped over her shoulders. She was shaking with a mixture of cold, fear, shock and whatever drugs she had been given by Teresa Savage, as Miller came and sat next to her.

"We must stop meeting like this," he said, voice deep and cracking with concern, belying the smile he was trying his best to muster.

Callie tried to smile back too, but she found her chin was wobbling slightly.

They watched as two white-suited technicians wheeled a trolley, loaded with a full body bag, to a plain grey mortuary van. Mrs Savage was leaving home for the final time.

"She was completely mad," was all Callie could say as a tear made its way down her cheek. "A monster."

"Is that your professional opinion, Doctor?" he asked, gently wiping the tear away with his thumb.

She did manage a better smile at that, and a sniff. He slid his arm round her shoulders and pulled her close. It felt nice.

"So, she killed both of them on her own? My body number nine and Michelle Carlisle?" she said into his chest.

"Yes."

She could sense that he had nodded and when he spoke, she felt the gentle vibration of the sound in his chest.

"Well, according to the Right Honourable Ted Savage, anyway." He was unable to keep the cynicism from his voice.

Callie had watched as the MP had been taken away in the back of a squad car, still white with shock.

"He says he knew nothing about the first death," Miller continued. "He hadn't even recognised the post-mortem photo we put out as being the person who had tried to blackmail him. Apparently, his wife said she had dealt with the problem and he assumed she had paid the boy off. It wasn't until she called him to help her with the girl's body because she couldn't manage to get rid of her on her own that he realised what had happened."

"Her brother helped too, with the clean-up, but I don't think he knew she'd killed anyone."

"No, he didn't. Jayne Hales worked out their relationship and we picked him up earlier. He'll get charged with arson and assisting an offender, but probably nothing more serious."

"And what about Ted?"

Somehow, despite the fact that he had happily taken part in orgies and drug-taking with young men, or in some cases, boys, and had helped his wife cover up the second murder, she still managed to feel concerned for him.

"Well, he's co-operating fully at the moment." Miller didn't seem to have the same feeling. "Although I have no doubt once his brief arrives, we'll be told his confession was coerced because he was in shock, but I think there's enough proof to show that he at least helped her move the girl's body. From that time, if not earlier, he must have been aware of what she'd done, what she was capable of doing. He will have to be charged with being an accessory."

"He saved my life."

"Yes, and I haven't forgotten that."

"And killing his wife was an accident. She fell down the stairs. He was just trying to stop her from braining me with the frying pan." Although Callie wasn't quite sure about that – there had been quite a considerable amount of force behind the push, hadn't there? More than was strictly necessary, but in the heat of the moment, who can say how much force is necessary?

"And I'm sure it will help reduce his sentence, but I'd bet my house that he'll still get a custodial sentence. There's no way round the fact that he knowingly helped his wife dispose of a body, even if she did tell him that she'd killed the girl in self-defence."

"She told me she just lost it and hadn't realised she had a kettle in her hand." But Callie didn't really believe that. The girl had been a threat to Ted and his precious career and Mrs Savage had removed that threat. Just like she had done with Daniel before her.

"Yes, well, we'll wait for your statement until whatever drugs she plied you with are out of your system. Don't want them saying you were off your—"

"Tits." Jeffries helpfully provided the word.

Callie sat up, suddenly; she hadn't even noticed he was there, and it seemed that Miller hadn't either as he quickly released his hold and moved away from her. She could feel a blush starting at her throat and steadily rising to her cheeks, and she could tell that Jeffries had noticed it too, by the way he was grinning.

"Your boyfriend called on your phone, Doc," Jeffries said and held out her mobile, which she must have dropped in the house.

"He's coming over to collect you, take you to the hospital for a blood test, so we know what she gave you."

"I'm pretty sure it was ketamine, same as body number nine," she said, trying to sound professional in front of the detective sergeant, but he continued to smirk, loving every minute of both her and his boss's discomfort.

Epilogue

The papers had been full of the case for weeks it seemed to Callie, and, inevitably, it was the story of the gay politician taking part in sex and drug orgies that dominated the headlines, rather than a man whose wife was prepared to kill anyone who stood in the way of his career.

There were endless discussions of why people in power put themselves in terrible positions, self-destructing so publicly, and every political sex scandal in history was rehashed for the readers and viewers.

"I think she actually drove him to it," Callie confided in Billy. "She controlled every aspect of his life. She was the one with the power, and we all know what power does."

They were watching yet another item on the news about Ted's glittering career and its end.

"Orgies are not the recommended way of taking back control of your life," Billy said drily. "Neither is killing your wife. Divorce would have been a better idea."

"She would never have let him get away from her so easily." Callie smiled. "You have to remember, this was everything she had ever dreamed of – position, status, power – albeit second-hand. She was prepared to kill to keep it. If he'd tried to divorce her, she'd probably have killed him."

Callie stroked his hand. Since the night he'd come to collect her at the scene of Mrs Savage's death, he'd seemed a little remote, as if something was on his mind, and she hadn't had the courage to ask him why. She wondered if Jeffries had said something when he answered the phone, when she was in the back of the ambulance with Miller. She knew the sergeant could be malicious, but somehow, she didn't think he would have done, after all, there wasn't anything to tell, was there? It wasn't like hugging a friend at a time of great stress was the same as being unfaithful, was it? Although, it had felt a bit like it at the time, she had to admit.

"What's up?" she finally asked, knowing that she couldn't relax until she knew.

"I've, um…" Billy seemed uncertain about what he was about to say, or about how she would react. "I've accepted a placement with a group practice. You know, one of the ones approved by the Home Office."

"Oh!" Whatever else, she hadn't expected him to say that. "Congratulations. That was quicker than I expected."

"Quicker than I expected as well." Billy seemed relieved to have finally told her. "I applied all over the place, thinking I would just go on a waiting list, but they came back straight away. I had an interview last week, well, a virtual interview, that is and they offered me the job."

"Just like that!" She smiled at him. "Where is it based?"

"Erm."

He shuffled his feet a little, hesitating before replying and she realised that the clue was in the fact that he had a virtual interview rather than a face-to-face one. It was somewhere far away.

"Northern Ireland," he said finally.

"Not an easy place to commute to," she said, a sinking feeling in her stomach as she went over the logistics of a long-distance relationship. Getting to an airport, flying to

Belfast. It would seriously reduce the amount of time she could be on call for the police. If not stop it entirely. Did she want to do it? Did she want to move with him to Northern Ireland?

"I know it's not going to be easy," he said by way of an apology. "But I need to do this, Callie. You do understand that, don't you? I need to go."

She did understand.

"And I need to stay here," she told him and could see that he had never expected her to up sticks, leave her job, her family and her friends to go with him. He had made the decision to go, knowing that.

"But once I have a few years' experience there, I can apply for posts in England. I won't be gone forever."

But they both knew that wasn't true.

THE END

If you enjoyed this book, please let others know by leaving a quick review on Amazon. Also, if you spot anything untoward in the paperback, get in touch. We strive for the best quality and appreciate reader feedback.

editor@thebookfolks.com

www.thebookfolks.com

ALSO IN THIS SERIES

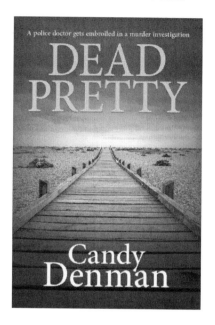

A police doctor gets embroiled in a murder investigation

DEAD PRETTY

Candy Denman

DEAD PRETTY – Book 1

When a woman is found dead in Hastings, Sussex, the medical examiner feels a murder has taken place. Yet she feels the police are not doing enough because the victim is a prostitute. Dr Callie Hughes will conduct her own investigation, no matter the danger.

Available on Kindle and in paperback

BODY HEAT – Book 2

A series of deadly arson attacks piques the curiosity of Hastings police doctor Callie Hughes. Faced with police incompetence, once again she tries to find the killer herself, but her meddling won't win her any favours and in fact puts her in a compromising position.

Available on Kindle and in paperback

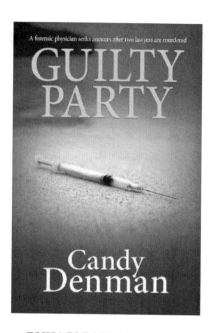

GUILTY PARTY – Book 3

A lawyer in a twist at his home. Another dead in a private pool. Someone has targeted powerful individuals in the coastal town of Hastings. Dr Callie Hughes uses her medical expertise to find the guilty party.

Available on Kindle and in paperback

Printed in Great Britain
by Amazon

55595910R00147